SIGNAL 99: FREEING FELICITY

A BROKEN HERO PROTECTOR ROMANCE

THE SIGNAL SERIES
BOOK 3

LC TAYLOR

You didn't break my heart. You freed it.

—STEVE MARABOLI

CHAPTER 1

Felicity yawned as she followed her co-workers into the parking lot. Dr. Borne smiled at her as he headed towards his car. "Thanks again, Felicity. We are thrilled to have you as part of our team."

It had been six months since returning to her hometown of Clinton. She'd swore she would never come back, but then her mother died, leaving her no choice but to return. Her mother left her the home she'd grown up in, giving Felicity somewhere to land. At first, it was hard to be alone in the house. The childhood memories were a painful reminder of everything she'd lost, and not just her mom.

"Well, thank you for letting me join the team. Y'all have been welcoming and have made me feel like part of the family."

"See you Monday. Have a great weekend." Dr. Borne waved as he got in his car.

Felicity smiled, giving the building one last glance as she opened her car door. Her smile quickly replaced her frown when her cell phone vibrated in her pocket. She knew who it was before looking.

Jasper.

He was just one more mistake in her life. When she moved home, Felicity was confident Jasper wouldn't want to follow her here—she was wrong; it turned out that Jasper wasn't willing to let her leave without him. Now, she was still trapped in a dead-end relationship.

Pressing the answer key, Felicity put on her well-practiced happy voice, "Hey baby."

"Don't fucking 'hey baby' me. Where the hell are you?" His tone was laced with the anger she learned throughout their relationship.

Felicity gritted her teeth and took a calming breath before responding. "What do you mean? I'm just leaving work, Jasper."

"It's almost seven, Felicity. Your shift ended nearly an hour ago."

"Jasper…" She pinched the bridge of her nose as she closed her eyes. "I'm a physical therapist. My last client was at six. *She* just left, and now I'm heading home."

He growled in response. "Get your ass home, Felicity."

Felicity held the phone to her ear long after he'd disconnected the call. Tossing the phone into the seat beside her, she pressed her head to the steering wheel. She wished Jasper would tire of this town and leave, but once they'd gotten here, he'd taken up with the 'not-so-good' guys she'd gone to school with. He could go out and drink with the boys, but she dared not ask to do the same. It would send him into a rage she'd rather not see again.

Felicity's house was about twenty minutes from the doctor's office she'd been lucky enough to get hired on with. She was the only physical therapist in the office, giving her job security. At first, Jasper didn't like her working for Dr. Borne, afraid he'd hit on her, but after learning Dr. Borne's husband was a fireman, Jasper relaxed. He still monitored her phone calls and expected her to give him her schedule.

Jasper didn't love her, not how he was supposed to—no, it was more about control. Her bank account helped, too. Not only did her mom leave her the house, but a nice-sized life insurance policy left her well off. Jasper siphoned her bank account while he sat on his ass. Pulling into the driveway, Felicity cut off the engine and took a deep breath. The house used to hold happy memories. Now, it felt like a prison. A prison she would never be free from as long as Jasper was inside.

"Jasper?" Felicity called out as she threw her keys on the entry table. "I'm home. Where are you?"

She walked through the house, expecting to find him—but only silence greeted her. Had she lucked out? Maybe he'd gone out, leaving her alone. After going room to room, confirming he was not anywhere in the house, Felicity ambled upstairs to take a hot bath. Her body ached from all the clients she'd worked with today. Rushing into the kitchen first, she grabbed a bottle of wine and a glass. Once she'd returned upstairs, she closed herself into the bathroom. The master bathroom, now hers, held an old-fashioned claw tub, something her mom insisted on putting in a few years back. Right now, she was thankful for the installation. Turning the spicket on, she dumped some bath salts and bubble bath under the running stream of warm water. Stripping her clothes, she set the wine bottle and glass next to the tub and climbed in.

The warm water felt amazing against her skin. Gripping the glass in her hand, she sipped the wine. Setting it down again, Felicity tipped her head back and closed her eyes. Pushing all the thoughts of how she ended up in this shitty place in life, she dozed off to sleep, wrapped in lavender-scented bubbles.

THE SENSATION of water covering her face caused Felicity's eyes to open. She struggled against the hand, holding her head underwater, finally pushing it free and jerking out of the water.

Sucking in a deep breath, *"WHAT THE FUCK!!"*

She wiped the suds from her eyes to find Jasper standing over her. He was smirking as he crouched beside the tub. "Enjoying your bath, Felicity?"

"Jesus, Jasper. You could have drowned me."

He flicked his fingers through the water. "Nah... I just wanted to wake you. Looks like it worked. Now get the fuck out of the tub and fix me something to eat."

Felicity sat up, covering her bare skin with her arms. "What time is it?"

"Almost midnight. Hurry your ass up. I have friends waiting downstairs, and we're hungry."

Jasper stood, storming from the bathroom and slamming the door. Felicity clenched her eyes shut, anger consuming her. He treated her like a slave, and she just wanted him to leave, to find someone else to control. Slowly, she pulled herself from the tepid water and dried off. Pulling on athletic shorts and a tank top, Felicity pulled her blonde hair into a ponytail and headed downstairs. She could hear the voices before she'd even entered the kitchen. Jasper was known to bring a friend or two over, but this time, a woman's voice was unmistakable. Rounding the corner, she saw Adam and Bruno, two regulars. Standing all too close to Jasper was a woman she'd never seen.

"Felicity, this is Alexis," Jasper smacked her on the butt. "She's going to be hanging out with us more often. Now feed us. We're all hungry."

Nodding, Felicity pulled open the refrigerator with a forcefulness that rattled the bottles inside. "Spaghetti, ok?"

"Yep—just make enough."

She began making dinner as Jasper and his friends sat around drinking. Now and then, she'd steal a glance at the men as they passed Alexis around on their laps. This was a new low, even for Jasper.

"Dinner's ready." Felicity watched as the men filed into the kitchen and sat around the table. Jasper smiled at Adam before pulling Alexis into his lap. Felicity saw red as she pulled the plates out and slammed them on the table. She served up each guest, finally stopping in front of Jasper. "Here, honey." She dumped noodles into Alexis's lap, who was comfortably seated on Jasper, followed by sauce. Alexis squealed, jumping from her perch.

"What the FUCK?" Jasper roared, jumping to his feet.

"It's one thing to order me to cook for your friends. But I won't stand here and watch you get handsy with another woman." Felicity threw the pan into the sink. "Enjoy your meal."

She turned, storming towards the stairs, but not before Jasper stepped in her way and grabbed her by the arm. "Who the fuck do you think you are?"

She closed her eyes and blew out a breath. "Let me go, Jasper. I'm tired."

"No. You don't disrespect me like that in front of my friends."

Felicity opened her eyes and glared at him. "This is my house. You and your 'friends' are free to get the fuck out. I'm going to bed." Felicity jerked her arm from his hand, wincing at the pain, and turned back towards the stairs. She didn't see the blow before it connected with her cheek, knocking her off her feet. Her hip connected with the bottom stair, sending a sharp pain up her side as she dropped to the floor.

"You won't talk to me like that. We're going out because I don't want to deal with your embarrassing attitude right now."

Jasper turned and left her crumpled frame on the floor. Felicity stayed huddled on her side, trying to understand what had happened. Jasper had never laid hands on her before. Usually, it was just the verbal and mental abuse—but he'd just crossed a line that Felicity struggled to comprehend.

Once Felicity heard the front door shut and silence filled the air, she pulled herself up to her hands and knees. Crawling up the stairs, she entered her room and pulled herself onto the bed. She knew she probably had a bruise on her hip and likely her cheek, but she couldn't look. Closing her eyes, she pulled the covers overhead and cried herself to sleep.

CHAPTER 2

Liam glanced around at his teammates as they sat shooting the shit at the local bar. He'd been the assistant commander for the Special Weapons and Tactics team for the last three years. Joining the police department right out of high school had been the best thing he'd done. Of course, he started in the tiny jail, but he finally went to the academy at twenty-one. He'd been working the road ever since. Being on the SWAT team was the highlight of his career. Even though there weren't many major incidents, any opportunity the team got to serve the city was good for him.

"You going to drink or nurse that beer all night, Sarge?" Bradley poked at him, breaking him from his thoughts.

"Fuck off, Bradley—not all of us have to drink ourselves silly to have a good time." Liam flipped his friend off as he tossed a peanut at him.

"I was talking to you, but you seemed lost inside that glass. Did you even hear what I asked you?" Bradley narrowed his eyes at him.

Liam nursed his beer. "No…sorry, what'd you say?"

"Damn, brother… you need to get laid. I asked you what you thought about visiting New Orleans for a guy's trip." Chase suggested, glancing at the guys.

Liam shrugged, "Oh—that. Sure… sounds like a plan."

"Yeah, maybe you could finally get your dick wet. You need to loosen up." Bradley laughed.

"Look, Bradley, just because I'm not a man-whore like you doesn't mean I don't get pussy. I prefer mine less used."

Bradley quirked an eyebrow at him, watching his reaction. "Pussy is pussy, Liam. Unless you're looking for true love."

Liam winced at Bradley's statement. The truth was, he refused to get close to anyone again. The last time he'd given his heart to someone, she crushed it when she left this town and never looked back. His mind immediately thought of his friend London and her recent wedding. Seeing Felicity at her house conjured up all kinds of feelings. He was not ready to deal with emotions. Glancing up at Bradley, "I don't believe in love."

"Well, I do. I'm going home to my wife." Arden stood and tossed money on the table as a group of girls burst through the entrance in a fit of giggles. He glanced at the door before pinning the guys with a smirk. "See you guys later—don't catch anything."

Finn looked over at the two of them and laughed. "Well, looks like your chance for some adult loving just walked through the door."

Glancing at the group, Liam shrugged his shoulders. "Fuck, Finn, they look like they're barely out of high school."

"Hey… legal is legal if they're over eighteen." Bradley chugged his beer and stood. "Ladies," he called out, turning towards Liam one last time. "You sure you don't want to hit on that?" He jerked his head towards the girls heading towards them.

"Nah—you go ahead. I'm heading out, anyway." Liam stood and threw some cash on the table. "See you tomorrow, Finn."

Liam watched as Bradley wrapped his arm around one of the girls. And though a small part of him wanted to go with them, the other part, the part that wanted something real, tugged him away. Finn, Bradley, and Chase could have fun without him. He wasn't interested.

LIAM PULLED into the house he'd grown up in. The walls held so many memories for him. As he shut off the engine of his truck, he saw his dad standing in the open door.

"Liam! What are you doing at home? Shouldn't you be out on the town?" He laughed, pulling him in for a tight hug.

" I have to work tomorrow, so I'd thought I'd come to chill out with my old man—I live here, after all."

"Who you calling old? I was just about to watch the game." Liam followed his dad inside. Pictures of his mom and their life littered the wall. His dad caught him staring at one of the many photos. "Your mom would be proud of you, Liam."

Nodding, "Yeah. I still miss her." Liam remembered the day she died. No one was expecting the call. She'd had a heart attack at the local grocery store. The clerk tried to do CPR, but it was a massive event—so the doctors claimed, trying to give them some reassurance, nothing could've been done. His dad was devastated, and for months, he walked around like a zombie. Liam feared losing him, too, so he sold his place and moved back home. Now, his childhood home was a bachelor pad. Well, if you could call it that. His dad didn't seem interested in dating, and ever since his high school sweetheart shattered his heart, he had no interest in dating. Sure, he fucked a few random girls here and there, but as soon as they got attached, he cut them loose.

His dad popped the top off a beer bottle and handed it to Liam. "So, what's new at the department?"

"Not much. It's been pretty calm lately—since London got shot, it's been like the town's gone silent."

His dad nodded, his eyes softening as he spoke. "That's a good thing, I guess… just means you're safe. How is she doing, anyway? She and that paramedic are married now right?"

"Yep. She's doing great. It's good to have her back, but I suspect she'll leave patrol at some point, you know?"

"Marriage does that. You want to ensure your partner is cared for—which means giving up things to ensure you'll go home to them." His gaze heated Liam's skin. It wasn't the first time his dad hinted at his concern over his job.

"Dad—" Liam started, but his dad threw his hands up, cutting him off.

"I know… but I worry about you. The world isn't as safe as it used to be."

"True, but this is Clinton. Not much happens here except—"

"For London getting shot." He sighed, taking a sip of his drink. "Oh… that reminds me. You'll never guess who I ran into."

Liam tipped the bottle to his lips. "Who?"

"Felicity."

Liam's ears rang so loudly he wasn't sure he'd heard his dad correctly. Gripping the bottle in his hand, "Who did you say?" He knew exactly who his dad had mentioned. Hell, he'd seen her himself at London and Davey's wedding but refused to believe it was Felicity—now he couldn't deny it.

"Felicity Jones. She's been back about six months. She works over at Dr. Borne's office as a physical therapist."

Liam shook his head. That meant Felicity had been London's physical therapist the whole time, and he never knew it—nor did anyone mention it to him.

"You know… your mom always thought you two would get married." His dad watched, waiting for his reaction.

Liam had thought the same thing once… until she ran away from town and never glanced back. "Yeah, well, people change."

"Liam." His dad's voice held a warning. "I don't know what happened between you two. Your mom would never let me ask. She said it wasn't my place and that you two were young and needed to learn life. But that girl was your sun. I just figured you'd know she was back."

Liam shot his dad a menacing look. He wasn't about to admit he'd seen her. That would lead to questions he wasn't ready to answer. "She left and never looked back. I don't think she ever really loved me. Maybe we were just too young to know what real love was."

"Bullshit—I saw how you two looked at each other. That was love. Maybe you should reach out to her… see what she says." His dad arched a brow, daring Liam to argue with him further.

Liam stood, downing the last of his drink. "Felicity is a history I'd rather not relive. Thanks for the beer, dad. I'm going to turn in."

"Son," his dad turned to watch him walk up the stairs, "Sometimes people run out of fear. It doesn't mean they love you any less—means they were scared."

"Thanks, Dad, but we'll have to agree to disagree on this one. See you in the morning."

Liam climbed the steps and shut himself in his room. Stripping his clothes, he stood under the warm spray of the shower. Bracing his hands on the wall, he closed his eyes and rested his head against the cool tile. His emotions were all over the place since learning he was right—it was Felicity he'd seen. His chest tensed with anger, but a tiny flicker of love burned beneath it. Felicity was supposed to be his forever girl… until she left him behind.

Turning off the water, Liam stepped out and dried off. Pulling on a pair of boxer briefs, Liam slid beneath the cool sheets of his bed. He stared at the ceiling for an eternity before finally falling asleep.

CHAPTER 3

MONDAY CAME TOO SOON. FELICITY STARED AT HER reflection in the mirror, trying desperately to cover the bruise on her face. She didn't feel like explaining the mark to her co-workers. She opted to pull her hair into a side ponytail, partially covering the purple marks near her hairline. Pulling on her scrubs and tennis shoes, Felicity headed downstairs.

Jasper glared at her from where he was standing. "When's your last client?"

"Seven tonight."

Jasper's voice was filled with an accusatory tone. "That seems late."

Felicity moved into the kitchen, keeping her eyes focused on her feet. She refused to let him see her fear as she blew a steadying breath and forced a smile. "It's a rescheduled client. She was supposed to come in last week but couldn't, and Dr. Borne asked me to stay an hour late to see her."

Jasper crowded her against the counter. "Come straight home after. You hear me, Felicity?"

"Yeah—I hear you." Jasper pulled her into his arms, placing a forceful kiss on her mouth.

Felicity kept the fake grin plastered on her face as she spoke. "I have to go." She hurried to her car, wiping at the teardrop that seeped from her eye.

As Felicity pulled into the parking lot, she checked her makeup one last time before leaving and heading inside. She quickly hurried past the front desk, calling out hello as she ducked into the locker room in the back. Glancing at her watch, she sighed in relief, knowing she only had a few minutes before her first client.

"Hey, Felicity." Lila came through the doors. "You ran so fast by the desk I couldn't tell you your first appointment was rescheduled."

"Oh—thanks." She glanced away, avoiding eye contact. "So, my first one is at eleven, then?"

"Yeah… hey." Lila sat down next to her and cocked her head. "Are you ok?"

"Why do you ask?" She kept her head angled away from her friend, trying to hide the black and blue mark.

Lila tapped her fingers across the smooth surface of the table. "Come on, Felicity. You stormed in here without saying hello, and now… you won't even make eye contact. Seriously, what the hell is going on?"

"It's nothing." She looked up, realizing too late, as Lila sucked in a breath, that she was putting the damage on display.

Lila made a clicking sound with her mouth. "That doesn't look like nothing. What happened?"

"I slipped in the bathroom and hit my head on the tub." Felicity stared back at Lila, praying she wouldn't press the matter.

Lila regarded her silently for a moment. "That's what you're going with? Look… I don't know what happens in your house, but if you're in trouble, I can help you."

Felicity fought back tears, praying her voice didn't crack. "No… I'm fine. Really, I fell."

Lila stood and headed towards the door, "Well since you don't have a client until eleven… Do you want to grab the office coffee? I could use some caffeine."

"Sure… I can do a run." Felicity stood, grabbed her purse, and headed towards the door.

Lila placed her hand on her shoulder, "Look… if you ever need help, I'm here. Don't stay in a bad situation, Felicity. There are too many of us here that care about you."

"Thanks." Felicity pulled her keys out, "Text me everyone's order. They can pay me back later." She headed out to her car, shame filling her veins. Her mom would be disappointed to know she was allowing a man to control her the way Jasper was, but she couldn't see any way out. He wouldn't just leave —even if she kicked him to the curb, he'd find a way to stay put.

LIAM SAT at a table in the back, sipping his coffee as he surfed social media on his phone. It had been a pretty slow morning, so he opted to get caffeinated at Charlie's, a local diner in the square. He was always on alert, his ears catching sounds that alerted him to danger. So, he was surprised when a voice from his past snapped him from his phone's screen. At the counter was the one person he never thought he'd see again.

Felicity.

She was just as beautiful as she was in high school. Her blonde hair was pulled to the side, but it caught the light just as it had all those years ago. He watched her as she ordered from Charles, the Diner's longtime owner, at the counter. Part of him wanted to go up and speak to her, but he stayed frozen in his seat. She hadn't noticed him, and he hoped it stayed that way because he wasn't in the frame of mind to deal with the past. Charles returned her change, and Liam watched as he leaned forward and said something that made her shake her head. Liam couldn't tear his eyes off of her, and as she gathered the trays of drinks in her arms, she flicked the hair that'd fluttered into her eyes, exposing the harsh purple bruise near her temple.

What the fuck.

Liam was out of his seat in a flash, his feet moving as if tugged by some unknown force to get a closer look at what he'd seen.

Felicity's head turned suddenly toward him, and she sucked in a breath. "Liam."

He stopped in front of her, his eyes flicking to Charles, who gave him a simple nod from behind the counter. "Hey, Felicity. Heard you were back in town." Felicity ducked her head, and out of instinct, Liam reached out and brushed away the strands of hair covering her face. "Felicity—what happened to you?"

She jerked her head away, but Liam could see she was embarrassed or hiding something from the blush that crept up her neck. "It's nothing. Wow…" Felicity let her eyes trail his massive frame. "Liam, I wasn't sure I'd run into you."

Liam clenched his fists. "Yeah—it was bound to happen." He could tell she was avoiding the question, but he would not let the massive bruise go and pressed on. "Now, can you tell me how you got the massive purple bruise on your face?"

"Oh—I fell in the bathroom. No big deal." She dismissed it, making his anger bubble.

"Bathroom? Felicity. Please don't lie to me. I've seen this too many times in my career. Is someone hurting you?"

"Liam," Felicity shifted the drinks in her arms, "It was nice seeing you. But I need to get these drinks back to work." She pushed open the door, leaving him to watch her make her escape.

Liam couldn't understand the tangle of emotions assaulting him as he watched her leave. He expected to feel anger, and he did, just not in the way he'd expected. He was angry at what he'd seen. She was lying about how that mark got there —he'd been a cop long enough to recognize the signs of domestic violence.

"Your gut isn't wrong, son." Charles jerked him from his thoughts. "Pretty sure that girl is tangled up with someone bad for her. That bruise on her pretty face doesn't lie."

Shaking his head, "What can I do about it? She said she fell."

Charles let off a deep huff. "Boy, you know as well as I do you won't let lying dogs lie."

Liam shrugged as he pushed into the sunshine. He needed to forget about Felicity and what Charles said. It was a road he didn't want to go down again. Getting into his patrol car, he stared at the space her vehicle occupied. Ignoring her was the right thing to do, even though he knew, deep down in his gut, he wouldn't be able to stop wondering if she was safe.

CHAPTER 4

Felicity minded the clock as she wrapped up her last client. She didn't want to be late—she'd catch hell from Jasper again. She was surprised to see him propped against her car as she walked into the parking lot.

"Jasper."

He walked towards her, grabbing her wrist and pulling her against him. "I thought I'd surprise you."

She tried to twist out of his hold. "Well… I'm surprised."

Jasper pushed her against the hood, wrenching her arm. "You been fucking around on me, Felicity?"

"What?" She looked him in the eyes, seeing a version of him she didn't recognize. "What the hell are you on, Jasper? I've been at work, you know that."

"Bullshit. A friend told me you were with a man at the coffee shop this morning. "

She blinked, confused who would lie to him about an inno-cent conversation with a police officer—who also happened to be her ex, but he didn't know that. "Who told you that?"

"Doesn't matter. So, answer me."

"No one—I picked up coffee for the office. I ran into an old friend... who is a cop. He simply stopped me and said hello."

Jasper pulled her hair, eliciting a wince from her. "Jasper. Please, you're hurting me."

"Get your ass home. You hear me? I gotta go pick something up. Don't go anywhere."

"Fine, Jasper. Fine." She pulled free and slipped into her car, watching Jasper drive off.

Putting the car in reverse, she backed out and headed home. The closer she got, the more anxiety she felt. She knew she needed to man up and tell Jasper to leave, but she feared he would blow up and make it difficult.

Pulling into the driveway, she knew it was time to end things with him before he killed her because deep down, she knew that's where this was headed. Felicity got out of the car and hurried inside.

Tonight, she would tell Jasper it was time to go.

She didn't want this life... and she sure as hell didn't want *him*.

JASPER NEVER CAME HOME, and Felicity finally gave up and crawled into bed. When she woke the following day, he still wasn't back. Part of her was relieved, hoping he'd freaked out learning her friend was a cop—but she knew it wouldn't be that simple to get rid of him, and he probably partied with friends.

Felicity headed into work, stopping again for coffee at Charlie's. She thought she'd surprise Lila and the rest of the office with caffeine to start their morning. Felicity had stayed off Liam's radar for six months, so she was surprised to run into him for the second time in less than twenty-four hours. Trying hard to get in and out without him seeing her, she pretended not to see him as she stepped to the counter.

She stood waiting for her order to be completed when she felt eyes on her. Glancing over her shoulder, she found his gaze fixed on her. She gave a half smile, relieved when Charles handed her the order. She thanked him and rushed outside, careful not to spill the drinks.

"Felicity." His baritone voice washed over her, creating a flurry of butterflies in the pit of her stomach.

Setting her drinks down on the roof of her car, turning, she forced herself to smile—despite the anxiety she was feeling being near him. "Liam. How are you?"

"I'm good. And you?" Liam seemed to peruse her body, looking her over with a watchful eye. Felicity was the same girl he'd loved all those years ago, yet she was different.

"Good as can be, I suppose. So… you're at the police department still?" Felicity couldn't make eye contact with him. She was still ashamed of how she'd walked away from him all those years ago.

"Yeah—since graduation." His tone was clipped as he answered. "I'm a patrol sergeant and team leader on the SWAT team. Heard you were a physical therapist—is that why you came back, Felicity? You swore you'd never step foot in Clinton again."

"Wow, straight to the point." Felicity fidgeted on her feet. As she tilted her head down towards her feet, her hair fell loose into her face. She knew this confrontation would happen eventually… just not in such a public place. "My mom died, and I needed a change."

Liam brushed the strands of hair from hiding her eyes from him. "Felicity… are you in some kind of trouble?" He could see the telltale signs of the faded bruise hidden beneath the rim of her sunglasses.

"No." She snapped. "Look, I'm sorry about what I did all those years ago. If I could go back…" the words died on her tongue. "Never mind. It was great seeing you again—but I don't need this trouble. I hope you can forgive me one day, but I get it if you can't. Lord knows I haven't forgiven myself, and I'm paying for my bad decisions now. See you around, Liam." She turned to get into her car, but Liam grabbed her arm.

"What do you mean you're paying for them now? If you need help or someone is hurting you, I can help."

She tugged from his arm, getting into the driver's seat.

Before pulling the door shut, she cast him one last glance. "I don't deserve your help."

Felicity closed the door, forcing Liam to jump out of the way. He watched as she sped from the parking lot, and he knew in his gut Felicity was involved with something bad.

As he watched her car fade into the distance—Liam knew she wasn't the only one in trouble.

He thought he'd buried his feelings a long time ago. Seeing the pain reflecting in her eyes, a familiar feeling bubbled to the surface… one that wasn't anything close to the one he'd carried around with him for the last couple of decades. Liam's heart stuttered inside his chest this time, and he knew it wasn't anger.

But what it was… he wasn't ready to admit to anyone, least of all himself.

CHAPTER 5

Felicity finished her day and hurried home. She was struggling with the emotions Liam brought to the surface—emotions she'd locked up tight years ago. Not long after she left, she realized Liam was the only man she'd ever loved. Unfortunately for her, that ship sailed the day she stupidly walked away. Seeing him two days in a row left her feeling confused. Felicity expected him to be pissed—maybe even yell at her. At first, she could hear the anger in his tone, but when he saw the bruises on her face, she saw the man she'd fallen in love with. He gave her the impression he wanted to protect her, but that was silly because she knew Liam would never forgive her for breaking his heart. The funny thing was, she'd broken her own heart, too. And now, sitting in the dark waiting for Jasper, she knew how much she'd blown her chance at a happy ending.

When Jasper finally came home, it was close to midnight. He came stumbling into the kitchen, the scent of alcohol permeating from his pours.

"Jasper, we need to talk." She rose from her chair.

He grumbled something under his breath before acknowledging her. "What do you need, Felicity? I'm tired."

"I'm serious, Jasper. This is important." She moved around the table toward him.

"Well," Jasper stared her down, "get on with it. I want to go to sleep."

She swallowed her nerves and spoke. "This isn't working."

"What isn't working?"

"You and me, Jasper," She closed her eyes. "I want you to leave."

"You want me to leave?" He moved behind her, gripping her hair in his hand. "That's it? You want me to go?"

He pulled the strands, causing her to cry out. "Ow, Jasper." She cried at the sensation of her hair being pulled by its roots.

He jerked her head, then slammed her down on the table. "I ain't going anywhere."

"Please… Jasper…" He tugged her hair harder, making her whimper in pain.

"You. Belong. To. Me. Felicity. Get that through your head."

Pulling her to stand, he pressed his lips to her neck, "Is this because I haven't been paying attention to you?" he ran his hand down her side and around her front. Slowly, his hand cupped her sex, pressing against it hard, "Maybe that's it, isn't it?"

"No… Please, Jasper. Let go. I don't want this."

"Don't want this?" He laughed. "Too bad. I want to get my dick wet, and you need to remember you belong to me."

Jasper grabbed at her scrubs, jerking them down to her ankles. She couldn't contain the cry that burst from her lips as he ripped through her panties and tossed them to the floor.

"Maybe this will help you remember who is in charge, Felicity." Jasper fumbled with his belt as he pressed Felicity onto the table.

She jerked against him, tears pooling on the wood beneath her chest. "Please, Jasper. Don't do this."

She couldn't stop the scream that tore from her lips as Jasper forcefully buried himself inside her. She pressed her cheek against the wood, gritting her teeth as Jasper grunted behind her. His thrusts were painful, practically ripping her from the inside out. Thankfully, as quickly as he'd begun, Jasper pulled free and spilled himself on her backside.

He released her hair. "Clean this mess up, Felicity."

Leaving her a wreck, Felicity collapsed to the floor in sobs. The cool tile pressed against her side as she lay in the mess Jasper had left behind. Her eyes were closing when his fingers dug into her arm.

Jasper grabbed her from the floor, pulling her body across the tile. "I told you to clean this shit up."

"Please… stop." Felicity sobbed, praying he would let her go.

She glanced up to look at the monster, barely recognizing the man she thought she once loved.

"I told you, Felicity. I ain't leaving."

It was the last thing she heard before his boot smashed into her face.

CHAPTER 6

LIAM SAT WITH HIS BACK AGAINST THE WALL. HIS SHIFT WAS about to start, and he just finished putting on his uniform when Arden walked into the room.

"Hey, sarge, why do you look like someone ran over your dog?" Arden slapped him on the back.

Liam sighed, glancing up at his friend and supervisor. "Hey, Lieutenant."

Arden cocked a brow at him. "Seriously, Liam, what's eating you?"

"Nothing, just lost in thought." He fiddled with his buttons.

"A girl then," Arden stated, nodding at his response.

Liam looked at his friend, wondering how he would know that. "What makes you think that?"

Arden shook his head, a slight laugh passing from his lips when he spoke. "When a man looks like you do, it's always because of a girl."

"It isn't what you think, though. I ran into an old friend yesterday and the day before. It was obvious she'd been beaten up, but she avoided the question both times and ran out on me."

Arden shrugged, slinging something into his locker and slamming the door. "You know how it works with battered women. Shame and sometimes fear keep them from speaking out."

Liam palmed the back of his neck. "Yeah—but that's not the woman she used to be. I can't believe she'd be taking crap from a man."

Arden moved toward the door. "Well, if you're worried, go check in on her. You know how to find her?"

Liam felt stupid… He hadn't thought about going by her work. "Yes."

"Then do yourself a favor and do a welfare check. Otherwise, your head will be out of the game—and you know how dangerous that is."

Liam nodded as he tugged his keys off his belt. "Fine… you're right. I'll ride over to her job later this morning."

"That a boy. Please let me know if we need help. Ok? And Liam…" he smiled. "You may not want to hear this, but it's apparent this woman means more to you than you're letting yourself realize."

Liam watched his SWAT commander leave the locker room. He was right. She was more than a friend, but his chaotic feelings confused him. She'd left him and broken his heart—so he didn't understand why it beat ten times faster when he thought about her. Maybe it was just unresolved anger and now concern for her wellbeing. Getting answers would settle his worry and perhaps clear up these crazy feelings.

LIAM PULLED his patrol car into the parking lot of Dr. Borne's office. Liam had been lucky enough never to need a physical therapist, but he'd been here once when London Brett needed a ride home. It shocked him that Felicity had been back for six months, and he hadn't run into her sooner—especially since he'd been by here and she was inside. He glanced around the parking lot and was concerned when he didn't see her car. Giving up, he went inside in hopes she got dropped off.

"Liam!" Lila called out as he approached the front desk. She was standing behind the receptionist, waving. "How are you? We haven't seen since London was a patient."

"I've been feeling pretty great."

"Then what brings you into the office?" She smiled at him.

Liam glanced around the interior, hoping to see Felicity. "I was hoping to speak with your co-worker, Felicity Jones. Is she available?"

Lila tilted her head and narrowed her eyes at Liam. "You and Felicity know each other?"

"Yeah, old high school friends." Liam didn't elaborate, but he could tell she wasn't buying his excuse.

Lila sighed. "I see. Well, unfortunately, she's not here. Her boyfriend called in and said she had the stomach flu."

"Stomach flu?" Liam frowned.

She shrugged, her tone changing to something that resembled disgust. "Well… that's his story, anyway."

Liam could detect the disbelief in her voice as she spoke about Felicity's boyfriend. "I take it you don't like him?"

"Never met him. But I don't think he's that nice to her. She's never allowed to go out, and the other day—you know what, never mind." Lila waved her hand in the air.

Liam took a step forward. "Wait, what were you about to say?"

Lila glanced around the waiting room. "Um, let's talk back here. Follow me." She pointed towards a door, motioning him to follow her. "Look, I don't know, but I think he may beat her," Lila spoke without a filter. "She came to work yesterday, and she had some bruises on her face—under her eye."

"Yeah, I saw those too." Liam ran his hand down his face. "We ran into each other at the coffee shop."

Lila's eyes narrowed on him. "Interesting."

He shifted nervously under her suspecting glare. "That's why I'm here. It bothered me all night, so I wanted to check in with her."

"Well, like I said. Dipshit called in for her this morning. It's weird, though."

Liam's brows furrowed. "What do you mean?"

"She never misses work. And the one time she was late, she called herself. It's bizarre that she wouldn't call in for herself."

Liam thought about her words and couldn't shake the feeling something might be wrong. "You got an address? I'll ride by and check on her."

"Yeah… I hope she's ok." Lila wrote something on a pad of paper and tore it off.

"Do you honestly think her boyfriend would hurt her that bad?"

Lila handed him a slip of paper. When he unfolded it, he smiled at what he saw. Felicity had been under his nose the whole time. It was like fate had been taunting them, waiting for the moment they would find each other again.

Lila hugged Liam before he walked out. "I don't know. Will you let me know what you find? Tell her to call me, please."

"I'll call you. Thanks, Lila."

Liam had a bad feeling in his gut, making the hairs on his arms feel like he'd been electrocuted. Closing his eyes, he prayed she was at home sick with the stomach bug—otherwise… he didn't know what he'd do.

CHAPTER 7

FELICITY OPENED HER EYES TO HER HEAD, SWIRLING WITH confusion. Blinking the haze from her vision, she realized she was lying in bed. Trying to roll over, something hard bit into her writs. Glancing at her arms, she nearly vomited when she saw Jasper had handcuffed her to the bed frame.

What the fuck?

Jerking her arm, she cried out. "JASPER!"

"Oh," he pushed open the door. "I see you're awake."

Felicity tugged at her bound arms. "Jasper… what the hell is the meaning of this?"

"You had a nasty fall, and I didn't want you tumbling out of bed." He laughed as he moved closer to her.

She shook her head and frowned. "Fall?"

"Yeah—don't you remember?"

Like a rushing wave, the memory of the night before came barreling back. She'd asked him to leave. Then he'd forced himself on her. The last thing she remembered was him kicking her. "I didn't fall. You know that, you bastard. Let me go."

"No… I don't think so."

She stared at him. "Jasper, work is going to be wondering where I am. You need to let me up. I won't say anything. Please… undo the cuffs."

Just as he moved to grab her, the doorbell rang. "Wonder who that could be. Here," he jammed a pair of panties in her mouth. "Don't want you making any sounds. I'll get rid of whoever is at the door."

Felicity closed her eyes, tears spilling down her cheeks as Jasper closed the door. Her cries were muffled by the fabric jammed in her mouth. Jasper had finally snapped—now she'd pay the price for letting the monster into her life.

LIAM STOOD on the front porch of Felicity's childhood home. He had so many fond memories of her on the porch. It's where they shared their first kiss, where they took pictures for senior prom, and where she broke his heart. Shaking himself from the reverie, he knocked again on the old wooden door. He could hear footsteps behind the door.

Slowly, the door cracked open, revealing a male around his age. "Can I help you?"

Liam shifted his stance, placing his hand on his holster. "I'm looking for Felicity Jones."

"Why you lookin' for her?" Jasper's gaze flicked to where his hand rested.

Liam eyed the man suspiciously, his gut churning with unease. "Her job was concerned and asked me to do a welfare check. Are you the boyfriend who called in sick for her?"

"Yeah—the boyfriend. Like I told them, she has a stomach bug. She's upstairs sleeping right now."

"What's your name?" Liam leaned forward, trying to peer inside the house, but Jasper narrowed the opening.

"Look, I don't see how that's your business, but my name is Jasper Hollings. Felicity and I have been together for two years."

"Right… I need to speak with her, though. To verify she is ok. Mind if I come in?"

Jasper moved his body in front of the tiny opening, blocking Liam more. "Yeah, I mind. She's asleep. When she wakes up, I'll have her call into work and talk to someone."

"Actually," Liam reached into the front pocket of his shirt. "Have her call me. It would make me feel better to hear her say she's ok."

"Fine." Jasper snatched the card from his hand and slammed the door shut.

Liam didn't like what he felt—he'd repeatedly seen this as a police officer. Something was wrong, but with no probable cause, he'd have to take Jasper's word. He sat in his patrol car, trying to search for Jasper in the system, but without his birthday, it was a shot in the dark. Liam called into dispatch, giving them what little he had, and then headed back to the doctor's office. He needed to chat with Lila some more. Maybe she or Dr. Borne had more information for him.

37

CHAPTER 8

Felicity struggled against the cuffs to no avail. She flopped against the mattress just as Jasper came back into the room.

"You'll never guess who that was…. It seems your co-workers called the cops." Jasper pulled a card from his pocket. "Seems a *Sergeant* Liam Carver—" Jasper tossed the business card at her. "Came by to check on you at their request."

Felicity tried to hide the surprise from her eyes. Liam had come here, and he'd been outside her house.

"So, here's what's going to happen, Felicity. You're going to call work. You'll tell them you're sick and will be out tomorrow. Tell them to call the police department and let this tool know you're fine. And if you give them any sign, you're anything other than sick…" he sat on the bed, wrapping his fingers around her neck, "Well, you don't want to find out. Do you understand me?"

Felicity's eyes widened as a lone tear dripped down her cheek. "Now, I'm going to pull this out so we can make that call. Ok?"

Jasper yanked the thin fabric from her mouth, causing Felicity to gag and cough. He pulled her phone from his back pocket and swiped the screen.

"Here, call your boss." Jasper pressed the phone against her cheek as it started ringing.

Felicity closed her eyes, praying she could keep her cool— because if she gave any sign, she was in trouble… Jasper would kill her.

LIAM PULLED his patrol car into the parking lot and got out. He couldn't shake the feeling he'd left her there in danger. Lila was sitting behind the desk when he walked inside. "Lila," he couldn't hide the apprehension written on his face. "You got a minute?"

"Liam, please tell me she is ok." Lila's voice was on edge as she stood.

"I don't know. Jasper answered the door and said she was asleep. But—" Liam rubbed his neck. "I didn't get a good vibe."

Lila led Liam to the back again; this time, she stopped in front of Dr. Borne's office, "Let's talk with Doc. I'm worried about her."

She knocked on the door and pushed it open. "Dr. Borne, you got a second?"

"Sure thing," he turned. "Liam Carver—What brings you into my office this fine day?"

"Doctor." Liam extended his hand, grasping his and shaking it firmly. "I'm here about an employee, Felicity Jones."

"Oh, yes, Felicity. Well, she's not in today—did she do something wrong?"

"No, I stopped by this morning to talk to her and learned she was out sick. Lila was concerned. I offered to go by her house and check. Her boyfriend Jasper wouldn't let me in to talk with her. Said she was asleep."

He shook his head, disgust marring his face. "Sounds about like him. He's a total control freak."

"What do you mean?"

Dr. Borne leaned back in his chair and held Liam's gaze. "Just that. He doesn't like her to socialize outside of the house. When she started working here, he initially freaked out over her having a male boss—then he met my husband at the fire department. Do you think she's in danger?"

"I ran into her at the coffee shop twice. I thought I noticed some bruises on her face, but she ran out when I asked about them both times."

He sighed, his head shaking. "Yeah—I noticed them as well. She told me she slipped in the bathtub, but I didn't believe her. I prayed she was telling me the truth. Damn… I should have pressed her more."

"I asked about them too. She told me the same thing." Lila twisted her fingers in front of her.

"Dr. Borne?" the receptionist came across his desk phone.

"Yes?" He held a finger up to us.

"Felicity is on line two. She's asked to speak with you."

"Thanks, Donna." He looked at Liam. "Well, this is interesting. I'll put her on speaker." He pressed a button. "Felicity, how are you feeling?"

"Dr. Borne," her voice was unsteady as she spoke. "I wanted to call and tell you I won't be in tomorrow—I'm afraid I am still feeling bad. I must have picked up a virus somewhere. I'm sorry about causing an inconvenience to you guys."

"No… No, don't you worry about that, Felicity. But do you need anything? Can I drop by some soup or medicine for you?" We could hear rustling in the background, and it sounded as though she whimpered. "No, thank you. Jasper is taking good care of me." Liam could hear the lies in her tone. "Can you please call and let Sergeant Carver know I'm fine? He came by today at your request. I was asleep."

"Sure… Sure… you think you'll be back in a day or two?" Dr. Borne asked.

"Um," it was apparent she was fighting back tears in the way her voice cracked. "I hope so. Maybe this is just a short virus. Look," she gasped. "I need to go. Sorry, guys." The call disconnected abruptly.

Everyone looked at each other with the same dumbfounded expression. "Dr. Borne, do you know if she listed any personal information about Jasper? Like a date of birth? I want to run him in the system. I don't have a good feeling. And Felicity sounded like she was ready to cry."

D. Bourne tapped his pen against the desktop. "She didn't sound good. Jesus Christ, what do you think is going on?"

"I don't know. Maybe he roughed her up a little, and they're trying to let the marks heal." Lila spoke, but in her tone, she didn't believe what she was suggesting.

"Look… I could lose my license by giving you this information, but I'm concerned for Felicity." Dr. Borne sat at his desk and keyed in something to his computer. He wrote something on a sticky note and handed it to Liam, "Here is his full name and birthdate. She had to list it for our life insurance to all employees. I'll deny you got it from me, though."

"Don't worry—I'll make sure your name isn't dragged into any mess."

He forced a smile. "Please let me know if you need anything else. Felicity has been a shining light since joining this team. Clients love her, and I'd hate for something to happen to her."

"You do the same. Lila," Liam turned to her friend. "Here's my card. You call me if she calls you or anyone else. I'm going to the station to talk to my supervisor. My gut is telling me something is going on. I don't know what."

Liam thanked the doctor and headed out. He needed to get Arden's take on the situation. Maybe he'd have some insight Liam hadn't thought of—because right now, Liam felt like he was racing against the clock.

CHAPTER 9

JASPER PACED THE BEDROOM AS HE RAN HIS HANDS THROUGH his hair. "What the fuck am I going to do with you, Felicity? You just had to fuck everything up, didn't you?"

"No, Jasper. We can fix this. Please, let me go. You can't keep me like this forever. Someone will eventually come looking for me. You know that."

Jasper turned towards her, his eyes wild and glossy. "You're not leaving this house, Felicity."

"What does that mean? Are you going to kill me, Jasper? Is that what you plan to do? Fuck… let me go, and we can just pretend this never happened. Please… I was just angry. I don't want you to leave." Felicity fought back tears as she tried to convince him of her lies.

Maybe then she could leave and find help. She knew this would not end well. He'd kill her. She was sure of it.

"No." His hand connected with her face, knocking her onto the bed. Her hand twisted in the handcuff; an audible snap echoed. Felicity couldn't contain the scream that tore from her lips.

"JASPER…" she sobbed. "My hand… please. I think you broke my hand."

Jasper ran to her side. "I'm sorry, baby." He ran his fingers down her hair, twirling them into her blonde locks, and jerked. "That was your fault. You did this." He glanced at her hand, now swelling and bruising. "I'll undo the handcuff. But if you try anything, it's going right back on. Do you understand me?"

Felicity knew she needed to remove the cuff before her wrist swelled around the metal. "Fine, yes. Please, take it off."

Jasper released the metal bands, freeing her hand, which she immediately laid across her chest. "Can I get some ice, please?"

"Stay put. I'll bring it up." He turned, pulling the door shut and locking her inside. Felicity stood, scanning the room for her phone. Disappointment filled her when she realized he'd taken it with him. She looked around for something to put on. Still only dressed in her scrub top, she desperately wanted some shorts to cover her bare butt. Jasper opened the door as she tried to pull on some athletic shorts.

"What the fuck are you doing?"

"Putting on shorts."

"NO!" he threw the bag of ice onto the bed and snatched her by her hair, dragging her backward. Jasper tossed her onto the mattress. "You'll stay bare for me. In fact," he grabbed her shirt, ripping it down the center and tossing it to the floor. "I want this off, too."

Felicity cried out, scrambling back until her back hit the headboard. "Why are you doing this?"

"You're mine. I told you that. And I want you naked—that way, you won't get any ideas to leave." He turned, pulling all her clothes from her drawers, and tossed them into the hallway. "Lay down."

"No… Jasper. Don't touch me—you lost that right when you did this."

"Oh, you think you have a say so?" Jasper grabbed his crotch. "Your sassy mouth is making my dick hard again. Maybe I should stuff it down your throat."

"I swear you try that, and I'll bite it off." She cried, drawing her knees to her chest.

Jasper smiled. "Well… there are other holes I can stuff it in." He grabbed at her legs, and Felicity fought, kicking him. Her heel caught him in the chin, causing him to cuss. "Fucking bitch."

He slapped her, knocking her head against the wooden edge of the headboard. "We can play hard. That's fine." Jasper turned, leaving her in the room momentarily before returning with rope.

"No, Jasper… Please don't do this." Felicity sobbed as he stalked towards the bed. "What happened to you… when did you become this monster?"

"The only monster in this room is right here," he cupped his cock. "And it's about to bury itself in your cunt." Jasper grabbed her legs, pulling her down on the bed. Looping the rope over her left ankle and tying it to the bed frame, Felicity fought against him, only to be punched in the stomach. She stilled as he pulled her right ankle to the side, tying it like he'd done with her other leg. She lay, legs spread wide, as he climbed on top of her, straddling her waist.

Felicity sucked in a sob as Jasper bent down and sucked her exposed nipple into his mouth. "I think I am going to enjoy having you like this." He swirled his tongue around the soft bud, pulling the pert tip between his teeth, and bit down. He pressed his lips to hers as he ran his hand down her hip. "Open that mouth, Felicity. You don't want to make me mad." Tears spilling down her face, she forced herself to kiss him back. His fingers traced her hip before he rammed them between her folds. She bucked against him, crying out against his lips from the painful intrusion. "That's it… you know you like this." Felicity turned her head as Jasper licked her neck, sucking and biting at her flesh. As he pumped his fingers in and out, the doorbell rang.

"Who the fuck is here now?" Jasper pulled his fingers from her cunt, smacking her ass. "Don't move." He laughed as he stepped from the room, leaving her tied to the bed like some animal. Jasper appeared in the doorway, but he wasn't alone. A man stood behind him she'd never seen before.

"What the fuck, dude?" The stranger said, looking at Felicity and then at Jasper.

"Felicity, say hello to Rob. Rob, this is Felicity. My girlfriend."

Rob stood, shocked. "Jasper—what the fuck are you doing?"

Jasper shot her a menacing smile. "She likes it kinky. Don't you, Felicity?"

Felicity turned her head to face away from Rob. "Rob, let's take a hit. Then you can watch me fuck her. She likes that." It all made sense now—Jasper was doing drugs. How had she not seen it before this?

"Alright, man, if you're sure." Rob's voice wavered as he shuffled on his feet. The sound of his boots scuffing against the wooden floor.

"Yeah—I'm sure." Jasper laughed as they headed out of the room to get high. Felicity closed her eyes, wishing for death. She was in hell. There was no other word for it. Karma had finally caught up to her—this was her penance for the heartbreak she'd caused Liam all those years ago. She made a mistake when she'd walked away from him—for what? A little freedom from this town? She loved him so much but worried she'd get stuck here. And now look at her—she was beyond *fucked*.

Her eyes grew heavy as she gave into sleep. Her mind swirled with memories of the night she ruined her life.

CHAPTER 10

Ten years ago

"Felicity, talk to me, baby." Liam ran his fingers through the golden curls, brushing her shoulders. He could sense something was wrong. She'd been pulling away since graduation.

She sighed against his embrace. "I don't know what to tell you, Liam."

"You know I love you. Whatever it is bothering you, we can work it out... together."

"Not this time, Liam." Felicity took a deep breath. "I got into college."

Liam leaned back and grinned at her. "Wow... that's amazing. I don't understand the problem."

"It's in Michigan, Liam." She held his gaze, the realization dawning on him.

"Oh." Liam stood, pacing in front of her. "Ok... We can make this work. I can get a job with a department there. No biggie."

"Liam." Her voice was filled with something he didn't like. "I don't want you to go with me."

Liam spun, "What do you mean?"

"I need to find myself. I don't want you to give up your dream and resent me, and I don't want to give up mine."

Liam stared at her, trying to consider what she was telling him. "What are you saying, Felicity?"

She fidgeted with her hands. "I'm saying, when I go to college, you'll be here. And I'll be there."

"Ok... so we do the long-distance thing. I can come visit on holidays." He shrugged, not getting the big deal she was making it out to be.

"No... you don't understand. I don't want you to do that, Liam. I'm trying to tell you I want to break up. It's the right thing to do. We're changing... growing up. You should see what's out there without a girlfriend in tow." She closed her eyes and took a breath.

Liam grabbed her arm, forcing her to look at him. "Are you crazy? Felicity—you're it for me. I don't need to see what's out there. I want to marry you. Have kids with you."

Felicity blinked as she held his gaze. "Liam, how can you know that? We're only kids. Hell, you just turned nineteen." Felicity watched as his whole body shook and tears spilled down his cheeks. Felicity's eyes welled with tears as she watched him. "I'm sorry. I love you, Liam, I do. But this is for both of us."

He turned, facing his car, "Good Luck, Felicity. I hope you know what you're doing."

Liam walked to his car, got in, and never looked back.

Even though she asked him to leave… inside, her heart was breaking.

———

FELICITY WOKE TO THE SOUND OF JASPER'S VOICE AS HE AND Rob came back into the room.

"Wakey, Wakey, Felicity." Jasper slapped her crotch, causing her to jump.

She cracked an eye, seeing Rob standing in the corner, staring at their interaction. "Rob here is going to watch while I fuck you."

She whimpered, closing her eyes to block out the terror. "Rob—you ready to see me tear this pussy up? God, I don't think I've ever fucked you high, Felicity. This is going to be good."

She heard his pants hit the floor as his belt echoed off the hardwoods. Felicity felt Jasper's hands against her skin, his fingers pinching at her center. "Look at that, Rob…" Jasper slipped a finger inside her. "She likes this. Never knew you were a voyeur, baby." He leaned over, running his tongue through her slit. "Mmmm, tastes as good as I remember. Open your eyes, Felicity. Look at Rob."

Felicity shook her head, refusing to do as he commanded. Jasper pinched her thigh, the pain forcing her lids open. "I said...*OPEN. YOUR. EYES.*" Felicity's eyes burst open as he grabbed her chin and turned her head towards Rob.

His friend stood against the bedroom wall. A look of disgust and concern covered his face. Felicity never broke eye contact as Jasper shoved himself inside her. It felt like her body was being set on fire as his cock filled her. Felicity's whimpers seemed to drive him into a frenzy, Jasper's thrusts getting faster and more violent. She watched as Rob turned his head away as Jasper pulled free, unloading his seed onto her belly.

Jasper stepped back and pulled his pants up. "That was fucking amazing. What do you think, Rob?"

"Yeah—it was fucking great. I need another hit, though. Call you when I get some more smack." Rob rushed from the room. Jasper stormed out right behind him. Once again, he'd left her tied to the bed. His fluids coated her stomach. Felicity let go, her sobs filling the empty room as she lay there, praying for death.

CHAPTER 11

Liam sat across from Arden, waiting for him to say something. Finally, he slid the file across the table. "That's a bad dude. Tell me again how you know her?"

Liam couldn't believe the record on Jasper. Surely Felicity didn't know… he couldn't believe she'd willingly date a man accused of the things in his file.

"We dated throughout middle school until graduation."

"Oh—high-school sweetheart's, huh?" Liam looked down at his hands, unsure how to answer his friend and boss. "Wait. Is this the girl that burned you? Making you steer clear of a relationship?"

Liam's head popped up. "Yeah—you could say that. But that's not important. Her co-workers are worried about her. And now that I've seen Jasper's rap sheet, I'm worried, too."

Arden leaned back in his chair. His eyes bore into Liam. "I can see why, but we can't just go charging in without probable cause. And calling in sick and a hunch isn't enough.

Maybe she'll call again or show up to work, and then we can intervene."

Liam tapped his pen on the table. "I hope that's not too late."

"Me either, but it's what we can do, Liam. Look, go home. Your shift ended an hour ago."

Liam tossed the pen down, scraping the legs of the chair across the tile as he stood. "Fine. We'll talk more about this tomorrow."

Nodding at Arden as he left, he couldn't shake his unease. Before he realized it, he was pulling into his driveway. Stepping inside, he was surprised to see his dad sitting on the couch. "Hey, Dad. Thought you had to work late tonight."

"Just got home ago. Bad day at work? You look like shit."

Liam filled his dad in on Felicity, leaving out no details. His dad growled as he looked at Liam. "You think this guy is beating her?"

"As much as I want to believe she's sick… yeah, I think so." Liam ran his palm over his face.

"Son, I know it's hard for you to sit and wait. But maybe she is sick. Give it a day or two, then check on her again."

Liam blew out a breath. "Yeah… maybe you're right."

"What else is bothering you, Liam?"

"I'm just confused. I mean… she left me, Dad. Said college and freedom were more important. I should be pissed still. But when I saw her the other day—with those bruises…"

His dad squeezed his shoulder and sighed. "Liam, you never got over her. I've watched you push relationship after relationship away. I knew it was because a part of you still loved Felicity."

"No—that's not it…"

His dad held his hand up, cutting Liam off. "Yeah… it is. You always looked at Felicity the way I looked at your mother. That, my boy, is love. I don't know why she needed to leave and find herself, but something tells me she never stopped loving you. Her mom told me a while back, before she died, how Felicity was in one bad relationship after another. I suspected she still loved you and couldn't find what you two had. Maybe this is God's way of giving you two a second chance."

"Dad… you're wrong. I loved Felicity. *LOVED* as in past tense. She shattered me when she left. I think I'm just remembering how things used to be. Worrying about someone you once loved is normal, even if that love isn't there anymore. I'm exhausted—I'll see you in the morning. Thanks for the talk, though." Liam headed towards the steps.

"Liam," his dad called after him, "Don't be scared to see your feelings for what they are."

Liam shook his head, climbing the stairs to his room. He hated hearing his dad's opinion, but was he right? Was he still in love with her?

It didn't matter. All he cared about was ensuring she was alright—everything else was just noise in his head.

CHAPTER 12

Felicity woke to the sounds of snoring. Her whole body ached, but she forced herself to open her eyes. Jasper was sound asleep on the bed beside her. His body pressed against her legs, which were still bound to the frame. She glanced at the table clock, noting it was nearly six am. Jasper's phone was charging next to hers on the nightstand. Felicity wondered if she could reach for the phone with her bad hand. She'd grit through the pain if she could get her fingers around it.

Jasper stirred next to her as his phone beeped with a text message. He snatched it up, glancing at the screen. "Fuck." Sitting up in bed, he pounded out a response and stood. "Don't go anywhere. I need to meet someone." He snorted a laugh as he looked at her. He pulled a t-shirt on and slammed the door closed behind him.

Felicity swore into the darkness. Turning her head, she couldn't believe her eyes. Jasper had left her phone. Felicity reached out towards the table, wincing in pain as her fingers brushed against the device. Her wrist ached, but she gritted her teeth and tried once more. Finally, the metal slid beneath her palm, allowing her to grip the phone and pull it onto the bed. She nearly passed out from the pain, panting as she bit her lip. She woke the screen, noting there was only twelve percent battery left, as she tapped out 911.

"9-1-1, what is your emergency." The voice filtered into the empty room.

Felicity winced in pain, forcing herself to speak. "Please. I need help. My boyfriend has me tied to the bed in our house… he's holding me against my will."

"Ma'am, can you tell me where you are?"

"Yes…I'm—" She was cut off as Jasper burst through the door.

"What the FUCK, Felicity!" snatching the phone, he hit end. "NOW YOU'VE DONE IT!" he screamed, smashing the phone into the wall.

Felicity clenched her jaw, closed her eyes, and waited for the blow. But Jasper only paced the floor. "What am I going to do, Felicity? They'll send cops now. You made a fucking mistake."

His fist connected with her cheek, causing her to black out.

<hr>

Liam sat at Arden's desk, contemplating what to do, when the Lieutenant's phone rang.

"Arden." He spoke, holding Liam's gaze. Liam watched as his brows knitted together. "You sure? Ok. Yep… I'll activate the team."

"What is it?" Liam watched as Arden swallowed nervously and took a deep breath.

"First, I need to know you'll put your job first, Sergeant." That fact Arden was using his rank and had gone into boss mode was a telling sign it wasn't good.

"What the fuck kind of question is that? Of course, the job comes first. What was the call about, Lieutenant?"

"Dispatch got a 9-1-1 call an hour ago. The call was cut off, but they traced the GPS coordinates from the cell phone. They sent a patrol unit out to do a welfare check…" Arden hesitated. "Liam, it's Felicity's house. Her boyfriend has her holed up inside and refuses to let anyone in."

"MOTHER FUCKER!" Liam jumped up. "Is she hurt? What do we know?"

"The officer on scene believes she is in the upstairs bedroom based on what dispatch discerned from the caller, who they believe is Felicity. Liam, she told dispatch that she was tied up to the bed before the call went dead. When the officer asked to make entry, the male on the scene refused him access."

Liam paced as Arden continued speaking. "The officer knocked again… this time, the idiot threatened to kill anyone if they came inside. He's really unhinged right now. The patrol supervisor on scene requested SWAT."

"What are we waiting for?" Liam headed towards the doorway.

"Liam, I need to know your head is clear and you can handle this call. I can't have your personal feelings fucking things up and putting anyone in danger."

His hand gripped the door frame, his knuckles tightening as he spoke. "I'll be fine. Let's go get this fucker."

He stormed from the office, bursting into the locker room. Liam was pulling his gear from his cubby when the others walked in. Hanson, Dingle, Chase, and Bradley started gathering their gear.

"Alright, team," Arden walked in. "We'll take the bearcat to the scene. The detective on the scene will establish communication with the perp and assess the situation. No one, I MEAN no one makes a move until we know what we are dealing with. Hopefully, this guy will cooperate, but based on the evidence so far, he isn't going to open the door and invite us in for tea. Any questions?"

"Nope—all clear." Liam snatched his gun and slung it over his shoulder. "Let's get on the truck… *now*."

"Hang on. Team, it's important you know this woman is a *friend* of Liam's. This is personal for him, so help him by following this to the letter. Let's bring her out safe and watch his back."

The team nodded, slapping Liam on the shoulder as they headed towards the bay. The bearcat sat idle as though it was beckoning them forward. They loaded up and pulled out of the station. Liam couldn't stop thinking about Felicity. He didn't know what happened but knew he'd stop at nothing to get her out safely.

CHAPTER 13

Felicity woke to the sound of Jasper swearing. "Fuck…" he kicked at the chair in the corner. "Wake up, Felicity. You dumb bitch… you did this. You brought them here."

She watched as he pulled her by the hair. "They're outside now. The cops."

He pushed her head back, slamming it into the mattress. She let out a whimper, which only caused him to rage more. "Hell no… you ain't gonna scream." He grabbed his dirty boxers off the floor and shoved them into her mouth. "SHUT UP!" He spat into her face.

Felicity couldn't stop the tears as they washed down her bruised and tattered face. Her whole body ached from the abuse Jasper had delved into her. And she could hardly see out of her swollen eyes.

Jasper pulled the curtain back. "What am I going to do…" he mumbled, running his hand through his hair. As he released the curtain, his cell phone rang. "FUCK…" Jasper kicked the door frame as he stormed from the room.

LIAM WATCHED as the detective on the scene attempted to contact Jasper. After calling back the number the 911 hang-up had come from, the detective had done some digging and found Jasper's number. Liam stood idly by, listening to the detective talk on the phone. His body language clearly showed that the call wasn't going as he'd hoped.

"Alright," The detective walked towards Arden and the team. "This guy is unhinged. He is refusing to come out and said the only way the girl is coming out is in a body bag." Liam bristled at his words, Arden casting him a warning glare. "Negotiations aren't going to work with this guy. I'll leave it to your team to decide how we proceed."

Arden turned to the guys. "Alright. You heard the man. We're up. We need to scout the place out and decide the best point of entry."

"I know this house like it's my own, LT." They spent the next ten minutes mapping the layout. Liam paced, eager to get inside, as his team gathered supplies.

"We'll get her, Liam." Arden gripped his shoulder.

He shrugged off his grip and stepped away. "Yeah… I know."

Dingle, their explosives and tech guy, slowly approached the house. He was setting up their pin camera and arming the door with explosives. The plan was to watch for Jasper to come back downstairs, then blow the door and rush into the house, taking him down. The wait was making Liam uneasy.

After what felt like hours, Jasper finally appeared in the living room. They watched on camera as he approached the kitchen, giving them their opening. The explosion was small but quick and efficient. As the team moved inside, Hanson, Arden, and Bradley headed towards the kitchen. A fury of gunfire erupted, followed by a mass of shouts.

Liam and Chase paused briefly before they rushed upstairs. After clearing the spare rooms, Liam paused outside the master bedroom and took a deep breath. They didn't know if they'd find her alive since the patrol officer on the scene heard what sounded like gunshots before their team arrived. Chase said something as he tapped Liam's shoulder and kicked the door open.

Liam burst through the opening, stopping dead in his tracks. Felicity was unconscious on the bed. Her legs and right arm were tied to the frame, as she was completely nude.

"LIAM!" Chase grunted, pushing Liam forward. The motion snapped him into action, and he rushed to her side.

"Christ," he slung his gun over his shoulder, dropping to his knees beside the bed, "Help me!" he screamed at his partner.

Chase went to work cutting the rope around her ankles while Liam freed her arm. He noted her left hand was swollen and a deep shade of purple.

"Felicity," he pulled his glove off, feeling for a pulse, "Come on." He grabbed his radio. "We need a medic in the upstairs bedroom, stat."

Chase had retrieved a blanket, slinging it over her naked body. "Fuck, Liam. What did he do to her?"

"I don't know." He ran his fingers down her hair, which was matted to her damp forehead.

"MOVE." Davey, Liam's friend and paramedic, barked as he dropped beside her.

"Jesus Christ, he really fucked her up. Come on, let's get out of their way." Chase pulled him from the room and led him downstairs. As they walked outside, they noticed Jasper's body lying in the middle of the living room.

"What happened?" Liam asked Arden as they headed towards the bearcat.

Arden grunted, "Fucking idiot pulled a gun on us. How about the girl?"

Liam closed his eyes as the visual of her broken form rushed to his senses.

"It was bad, LT," Chase said. "I'm pretty sure he assaulted her. She, for sure, has a broken arm. *Fuck…* that mother fucker left her laying there in her own fluids, and God knows what else."

"Someone needs to call her employer. They're the ones who called this in. She's a nurse?" Arden asked, turning towards Liam.

"No, physical therapist. She's the one who rehabbed London Brett." Liam stripped his vest off and tossed it into the back of the truck. "I'll call Dr. Borne. Her co-workers are the only family she has right now… she's going to need them. LT, can I…"

Arden cut him off. "Liam… I know the history—and as I said earlier, you've got some unresolved feelings for her. It isn't a stranger's face she will want to see if she wakes up. Go with the medics to the hospital. I'll send Chase by later to get you."

Liam jogged towards the ambulance, where Davey loaded Felicity into the back. Liam recognized one of the firefighters on the scene as Dr. Borne's husband, which meant he likely called him already. Liam stared down at the only girl he'd ever loved and wondered how she'd gotten herself to this point in life.

"She's got a strong pulse, Liam." Davey reached out and rested his hand on Liam's arm. "And knowing how she busted London's balls during PT, Felicity's a fighter."

Liam finally took in the paramedic's expression. Davey knew Felicity too—maybe not as well as Liam, but it didn't change the fact that he was seeing someone he knew on a personal level.

"Thank you, Davey."

Davey gave a slight nod of his head and turned back to Felicity.

Liam watched and prayed—needing her to be ok.

CHAPTER 14

Liam paced the tiny hospital room. The doctors had immediately taken her to radiology for a scan. They were concerned she had a head injury based on the visible trauma and the fact that she hadn't regained consciousness since arriving. The door burst open as Lila rushed in. "Where is she?" Her frantic tone made Liam stop in his tracks.

He turned toward the window, trying to compose his rage. "Still upstairs. They're running some tests and still have to do a…" Liam clenched his fists and gritted his teeth. "Rape kit."

Lila gasped, causing him to turn and face her again. He realized her eyes were brimming with tears. "Hey," he stepped close and wrapped his arm around her shoulder. "She's alive. That's all that matters right now. We can help her with the rest later."

As he hugged her, the doctor stepped in, forcing Liam to release Lila and step away. "Doc, any update?"

"Sergeant." He motioned to them, to the two of them. "Are either of you family?"

"No, sir. Felicity doesn't have any family left. She and I, well, we were close growing up. I guess…"

Lila cut him off. "She has me too. I'm her friend and co-worker—she's like family to all of us."

"You work with her?" the doctor faced her.

"I'm Lila… Felicity and I work together for Dr. Borne. She's the physical therapist at our office."

"Oh. I know Dr. Borne." He seemed to think for a moment. "Felicity is going to need some help…" He rubbed his chin and took a steadying breath. "She suffered an exuberant amount of trauma. Her left wrist was broken—it appears she had been cuffed after the fact. She might have some nerve damage, but we won't know until the swelling goes down. Her cheekbone was fractured, as well as her right orbital. We don't think there is damage to the eye, but again," he paused. "We just don't know. Not until she wakes up."

"When will she wake up?" Liam studied the doctor.

"It could be days or hours. She suffered several blows to the head… her brain is trying to recuperate."

Liam blew out a breath in frustration. "Jesus Christ. It's a good thing that fucker is dead."

"I'm afraid there's more." Lila glanced at Liam, and they shared a worried expression as the doctor continued. "It appears he sexually assaulted her several times. She has some internal injuries consistent with rape."

Liam roared in anger as Lila's sobs echoed through the room.

"The bizarre thing is that he seemed to have preferred to mark her instead of finishing inside of her—at least that's what the rape kit showed. She had no semen internally, just all over her."

"So, you're saying that sick son of a bitch dumped his bodily fluids on her?"

"Yes. We've cleaned her up. We also gave her some medication as a precaution—But it doesn't look like there is a great risk of pregnancy. Look, Liam, Lila," he sighed. "She is going to need friends to help her through this. She'll need someone to stay with her for the first couple of weeks once she's released. And someone will need to encourage her to see a therapist." He glanced at his cell phone. "She's done upstairs. They'll be bringing her down in a few minutes. I've got to talk to the detective. Let the nurse know if you have any other questions. Either way… you two need to prepare yourselves. She doesn't look like the Felicity, you know."

CHAPTER 15

Felicity wasn't sure where she was. She only knew her whole body hurt… *badly.*

"Felicity?" someone was speaking, though it sounded like they were in a tunnel. She tried to open her eyes, but they were weighted down by lead. "Can you hear me?"

"Yes…" Her voice didn't sound like her own.

"Don't talk. Just nod."

She forced her lids open to tiny slits. The light burned her retinas, making her wince in pain. As her vision cleared enough to make out her surroundings, she was shocked to find Liam beside her bed. Lila stood at her feet, watching her with a cautious expression.

"Where am I?" Her throat was raw, as if glass shards had been shoved down her esophagus.

Lila's voice filled her ears. "You're in the hospital, Felicity."

The hospital.

Felicity blinked—at least, she tried to blink. Pain radiated down her jaw as flashes of memories assaulted her.

Jasper.

She inhaled, her eyes darting wildly around. "Jasper?"

"Oh, Felicity." Lila sat on the bed beside her, taking hold of her hand. "He's gone."

A sob bubbled up, erupting from her chest. "Don't cry. You need to rest. We'll be here when you wake up, Felicity. Everything's going to be alright."

Felicity closed her eyes again. The medication seeped into her veins, carrying her away from the pain lancing through her, deep to the bone.

LIAM WATCHED as Felicity drifted off to sleep.

"I should have done something more," Lila's eyes misted.

"What?" Liam cut his eyes toward her. "What could you have done? She was too ashamed to tell anyone he was doing this to her. If anyone should blame themselves, it's me. I saw the bruises. And I'm a fucking police officer. But I let her walk away because I refused to let myself become involved with her again."

Lila shook her head. "No, you're right. This isn't anyone's fault—well, only Jaspers. Do you think…" She swallowed, "Do you think she will make it through this?"

"I don't know, Lila. This is going to be the hardest thing she's ever faced." Liam sighed, his hand squeezing the tender flesh above his nose. "Look, I don't want to leave her here, but I need to check in at the station and talk with my Lieutenant."

"Don't worry. I'm not going anywhere. Dr. Borne wants me to stay with her until we know what's going to happen to her."

"Ok. You have my number. Call me if something changes or she wakes up."

Liam hugged Lila as he cast one last glance at Felicity before leaving the room. His mind played over the events repeatedly. He'd known something was off the day he saw her at the coffee shop. All Liam could think about was how he walked away… maybe if he'd pressured her more about it, she wouldn't be laying in a hospital bed.

CHAPTER 16

FELICITY SLOWLY CAME TO… THE LIGHT WAS LESS PAINFUL AS it shone in her irises. The soft beep of machines and the steady sound of people moving about reminded her she was in a hospital. Turning slowly to the side, she found Lila asleep in the chair.

"Li…" she tried to say her name, but her voice was horse.

Lila stirred as the door to the room opened, illuminating the hallway behind a nurse who entered. "Well… look who's awake."

"I," Felicity whispered.

"No… no. Don't talk, sweet girl. Let's check your vitals." The nurse moved around her bed.

Lila stood, moving to stand beside her as the nurse worked. "Felicity. Thank god." She gently pulled Felicity's hand, which was covered in a bright pink cast, into her hand. "Your wrist was broken. Do you remember anything, Felicity?"

Felicity clenched her eyes shut, wincing in pain. She wished she could say no, but she remembered everything—well, almost everything. Some parts were fuzzy—like how she'd gotten here. Just as she opened her eyes, a flash of Liam's face filled her head. He had been there… He'd seen her tied to the bed like an animal.

A tear slipped free and spilled down her cheek.

"No—please don't cry." Lila wiped the lone drop from her skin. "You're safe now. He's gone, Felicity. He can't hurt you again."

Felicity nodded her head as best she could. "Liam?" she forced his name out between her lips, the words painful for several reasons.

"He was here last night. I told him I'd call, but I am sure he'll be by this morning."

"*No.*" She rasped.

"No?" Lila questioned. "Felicity, he will want to see you're ok."

"No… please. I don't want him to see me like this." Her voice was low, barely audible, as the words rushed out.

"Now, darling," the nurse pulled the stethoscope from her ears. "That man was mad as hell to leave you here. I am sure he'll need to see you awake with his eyes."

"No." She cried, the tears pouring out as she tried to plead. "Don't let him see me like this. *Please.*"

"Felicity," as Lila pleaded with her, the door opened, revealing the man himself.

Lila cast Liam a look of sadness and worry. "Shit."

"What is it?" Liam rushed inside, gasping, when he saw Felicity was awake. "Felicity." He muscled Lila out of the way so he could stand beside her bed. "You're awake, thank God."

Felicity turned her head away, ashamed to look him in the eyes. "No...*go*." Her voice cracked as she spoke the words.

"What?" Liam looked at the nurse. "What'd she say?"

"Liam," Lila whispered his name. "She said she didn't want you to see her like this."

"Why? Felicity?" he turned to her, his heart beating wildly. "Is that true?"

"*Please.*" She sobbed, the machine beeping in response to her pressure rising.

"Look," the nurse placed her hand on his shoulder. "I think you should go. Getting upset like this is not good for her right now. Give her some time."

Liam stood, "Felicity—It's me. Please."

"Just go." She muttered between sobs.

Liam cast a glance at Lila, his eyes filled with hurt. "Will you call me when she's ready?"

Lila nodded, regret and sympathy lacing her glistening eyes. This was going to be hard on everyone, Liam included. "Felicity, I'll leave. But I'm here for you. Please don't shut me out."

Liam walked out of her room, wincing when the door closed behind him. He didn't understand why she was pushing him away. Shaking his head, he decided he needed to talk to someone, so he headed home. His dad would know what to say—or do… about Felicity.

Liam would give her space for now, but he wouldn't stay away forever.

He was relieved to see his dad was home as he pulled into the driveway. If anyone could help him make sense of his feelings, it was him. Hank Carver was a solid man and a great father.

Liam hurried inside, tossing his keys onto the table. "Dad?" he called out.

"In here." He heard his voice call out from the kitchen. Liam plopped down into a chair as his dad finished making himself something to eat.

"What brings you by this morning? Shouldn't you be out making arrests?" His dad chuckled as he sat down opposite Liam.

"I need some advice."

He shifted in his seat, turning to Liam. "Well shit, this must be serious if you're coming home in the early morning to ask me for advice."

"It's about Felicity."

He grinned. "I knew you two would find your way to each other eventually."

"No, Dad. It's not like that. We worked a call last night… a hostage situation."

His dad set his fork down. "A hostage situation? What's that got to do with Felicity?"

Liam took a deep breath. "It was her, Dad. She was being held against her will by her boyfriend."

"Holy fuck. Is she ok? What the hell, Liam."

"She's in the hospital. We got her out, but it's bad, Dad. Real bad." Liam fought to hold his emotions in. "He's dead. He tried to shoot at us when we made entry. But Felicity—" his voice wavered. "He'd done awful things to her. She was tied to the bed like an animal. Bruised and battered, Chase had to cut the ropes... I," tears welled up in his eyes.

He hadn't noticed his father had stood and moved beside him. "I should have done something... we ran into each other earlier in the week, and I saw the bruises. But she lied and blew me off." The tendrils of salty water splashed down his skin, wetting the table. His dad's arm wrapped around him, pulling him into a hug.

"Liam... this isn't your fault. My guess is she was embarrassed to admit to *you,* of all people, she was in a bad situation."

"She looked so fragile, Dad. So broken." Liam sobbed into his dad's shoulder. "She won't let me see her."

His dad's arm tightened around him. "What do you mean?"

"She asked me to leave the hospital."

"Oh, Liam." His dad patted his back. "She's got to be ashamed to be seen like that. Especially by someone she probably still has feelings for."

Liam sucked in a breath. "That's stupid, Dad. She can't possibly have feelings for me…"

"If you say so. Either way, that woman doesn't want you to see her as a broken bird. Her dignity has been ripped from her. Give her time, son. Plus, you need to sort out your feelings."

Liam lifted his head to look at his dad's face. "My feelings?"

"Yes. Your feelings. I suspect this situation bothers you because you still harbor unrequited love for her like I've been saying."

"No." Liam stood. "I'm just worried about her. She has no family left. How is she going to get through this alone?"

"Oh, Liam, my boy. You'll figure it out in time. But all you can do is to be there on her terms."

"Yeah, sure." Liam headed towards the steps. "I'm off today because we were out so late on that call. I need to get some sleep."

"Sure thing. I'll wake you for dinner." His dad laughed, "Liam,"

"Yeah," Liam glanced over his shoulder.

"When someone you love hurts you, you make yourself believe you don't love them anymore. But when it's the real thing, love doesn't disappear. Sometimes, you need something big to trigger those feelings again. Just keep that in mind when you think about Felicity. You two were good together. I think she just got scared. Hell, you were only 18, so it makes sense. Plus, when you're young, you do dumb things."

Liam nodded, thinking about what his father said as he headed upstairs to sleep. He couldn't still love Felicity, could he? But as he thought about what she'd gone through, his heart squeezed painfully inside his chest. He cared about her, that was certain, but love? His pulse quickened with the word as it rolled around in his head.

Did he still love Felicity?

Closing his eyes, he pictured her face, and his heart did a flip-flop. His dad might be right.

Shit… he was in trouble.

CHAPTER 17

Felicity could not believe she'd been so stupid. Jasper nearly killed her. Lila stood beside the bed, holding her hand in hers.

"Look… I know you're embarrassed, but you didn't do this, Felicity. The only person to blame is Jasper. Do you hear me?"

Felicity couldn't respond. She let the tears fall unabashedly down her face, a face that was swollen, bruised, and disfigured. God, how she must look to Liam—the shame ripped through her veins at lightning speed, forcing another howl from her chest.

"Good morning. Glad to see my patient is awake." The doctor walked in, giving Felicity a timid smile. "Let's look you over, shall we?"

He checked Felicity, inspecting her cheek and eyes and finally taking her vitals. "Everything sounds and looks good, but Felicity, I need to ask you something," he pulled a chair to her side. "When you were brought into the hospital, there was apparent trauma we took care of… then there is some less obvious stuff. Jasper assaulted you—but it appears he never… how do I say this delicately?" The doctor glanced at Lila, who placed her hand on Felicity's shoulder. "Felicity, your body was covered in bodily fluids, but it didn't appear there was much inside you. As a precaution, though, and since it was forced relations, we gave you some medicine to prevent pregnancy."

Felicity squeezed her eyes shut. Jasper had forced her several times, not just when she was tied to the bed, and even though she'd been on the pill since high school, she'd missed a few over the last few days.

"You will cramp and probably bleed. It forces your body into a menstrual cycle in most cases. We also need to discuss your care. You cannot be left alone for at least two weeks. We'll keep you here for one of those weeks to ensure your eye socket and cheekbone are healing properly. If they are healing to my satisfaction, I'll release you—BUT only if you have someone at home to help you. So, take the next couple of days to work that out, ok?"

She nodded, "Can I sit up?"

"Of course." The doctor helped her adjust the bed to a seated position. "The catheter can come out today if you feel stable enough to walk to the bathroom."

Felicity noticed the bag hanging off her bed. "Please… my legs are the only things that seem to work normally." She winced as her face throbbed in response to talking so much. Her voice was becoming clearer, but the downside was the pain she had to speak through.

"Alright, you press that button if you need anything—pain meds, whatever… And Felicity," the doctor placed his hand on the doorjamb. "I want you to talk with someone—the hospital psychologist will probably stop by this evening."

She nodded, knowing it was something she would need to do for him to send her home, anyway.

"Dr. Borne wants to stop by," Lila broke the awkward silence. "His husband was one of the firefighters on the scene when they killed Jasper."

"Oh." Felicity didn't want anyone to see her like this, but she knew he was a stubborn man who wouldn't take no for an answer. "He can come by."

"But not Liam?" Lila asked quietly.

"No." Felicity gasped.

"Fels, why? That man was beside himself when they brought you in… he obviously cares about you. What's the story there?"

Felicity smiled at her friend. Memories of Liam assaulted her brain, causing a sharp pain to settle in her chest. "He was my first… and only love. And I, the idiot I am, broke his heart to sow my oats. Look where that got me."

Lila frowned at her words. "Wait… what do you mean you're only love? You were with Jasper for over two years, right?"

"Yeah—but I asked him to leave the night he flipped out. I knew it wasn't love. He was a controlling monster, and when he started using it got even worse. But Liam…" Felicity looked out the window and back to Lila, "He took my heart back then, and when I saw him a few days ago, I realized I never got it back. Shitty relationship after shitty relationship —I finally accepted he was the only one who I ever wanted." Sighing, "When I left for college, I told him I didn't want to do the long-distance thing. I broke that man's heart—I don't deserve his help."

"Look—you were what, eighteen? That was ten years ago, Fels. You were just a kid… hell, he was just a kid. I don't know Liam well, but he's been the eternal bachelor. Turning down anyone who's tried to get in his bed. I'm not even sure he does random hook-ups. That has to say something. And the way he looked at you… it wasn't a man looking at a woman like she was broken. No, he was looking at the woman he loves."

"There is no way he loves me. You have that wrong."

Lila smirked as she rolled her eyes. "Well, we will see about that."

Felicity and Lila fell into a generic conversation after that. Dr. Borne and his husband stopped by and sat with her for several hours. Everyone was grateful she hadn't been killed, and Dr. Borne assured her she would still have a job when she returned. Felicity laughed because she would likely need physical therapy on her hand when she got the cast off. One thing stuck out from their conversation, though… Dr. Borne mentioned Liam and how he had some unresolved feelings for her. He and his husband, who saw Liam on the scene, agreed that Liam and Felicity needed to talk.

Felicity wasn't surprised when Davey and London walked through the door a few minutes after Dr. Borne and his husband left.

"Felicity." London rushed to her side and held her in a soft embrace. "I'm so sorry I didn't realize what was happening."

"London. You can't blame yourself—I hid it from everyone." Felicity blew out a breath. "Davey." She turned to the paramedic and friend who brought her in. "Thank you for being the one who got me here."

"I was terrified, Felicity. Seeing you—" He shook his head. "Not to mention Liam. He was a basket case the whole ride to the ER. That man loves you something fierce. How did we not know you two were together?"

Felicity glanced at her friends. "We aren't. Not for a long time, anyway. He didn't even know I was back until a couple of days ago."

"How's that possible?" London cocked her head. "He was at our wedding. How'd you not run into him?"

Felicity sucked in a shocked breath. "I… I don't know. But we aren't together. I fucked that up a long time ago."

"Could have fooled me." Davey smiled. "Pretty sure you're both in denial."

They fell into a normal conversation after that. Felicity was surprised they'd come to see her, but she was grateful. As they left her to her thoughts, Felicity couldn't help but replay Davey's words. *You're both in denial.*

Felicity couldn't cling to that notion only to get hurt, so she pushed it out of her mind—it didn't matter if it was true. Felicity didn't want him to see her broken.

She reiterated to the nurse… Liam was not allowed in her room.

CHAPTER 18

Liam paced in the locker room, anger filling his veins. Felicity refused to let him see her, yet everyone else had free passes into her room. The nurse had stopped him when he went by the other day, telling him emotionally she wasn't ready to see him yet. She assured him that would change and to give her time, but it pissed him off, anyway.

"Whoa, Liam," Hanson slapped him on the shoulder, "Calm down—you're pacing like a mad bull in a China shop. Who do you want to kill right now?"

"Felicity won't let me see her."

"Ah… I get it now." Liam stopped moving, turning to pin his partner with a ferocious glare. "You're in love with that woman and stewing with anger that she won't let you in."

Liam glared at his friend. "What? NO… I need to see her, and she's being stubborn about it."

"No… you're in love with her. Didn't you say she was someone from your past?"

"Yeah… she and I—we dated most of middle and then high school. I thought she was the one I'd marry, then she broke it off and left for college."

Hanson sat down on the bench. "I see."

"What do you see?" Liam plopped down next to him.

"You never stopped loving her. Sure, you might have been pissed as hell at her, but your heart always belonged to her. That's why you've never had a serious relationship."

Liam grunted. "What the fuck, Hanson. You, Dr. Phil, now?"

"Nope… it's just obvious to everyone but you. You. Love. Her. Now—what the hell you going to do about it?" Hanson stood. "Shifts over. Go see her, and don't take no for an answer."

LIAM PARKED in the visitor lot—Hanson and his dad insisted he still loved her… Did he?

He knew he needed to see her if he was ever going to figure it out. It'd just about driven him out of his skin over the last week, unable to put his eyes on her. He wasn't taking *no* for an answer today.

"Liam," the nurse met him outside her door. "You can't go in there. Let me see if she's willing yet.".

Liam paced the hallway, his shoulders sinking when he saw the nurse emerge with a deflated look. "She's not ready. I'm sorry."

Grabbing a nearby chair, "Well, then I'll wait. Let her know I am sitting outside her door until she agrees to see me."

The nurse laughed, shook her head, and disappeared inside Felicity's room. When she came out, she tried to stifle her grin, but failed. "She said she hopes your butt is padded."

Liam couldn't resist the laugh that bubbled up—at least her sarcasm was returning. That was a good sign, in his opinion. Liam kicked back and closed his eyes. He must have dozed off because he was startled awake when he heard her door open and a man step inside. The hairs on the back of his neck prickled as he stood. Stepping to the closed doorway, he leaned in to listen.

<hr>

"FELICITY?" a smooth-sounding voice penetrated Felicity's slumber. Liam must not know what stay away meant.

"Liam, I thought I told you to stay…" Her voice froze on her tongue when her eyes landed on the man standing at the foot of her bed. "YOU! NO GET OUT! GET OUT NOW…"

"Please… I wanted to tell you," Rob pleaded as the door to her room burst open. Felicity shot a frightened glance towards Liam, whose eyes showed murderous rage.

"Felicity?" Liam questioned, looking from her to the man at the foot of her bed.

"Please… get him out of here." She clutched the covers to her chest, and crocodile-sized tears billowed down her face.

Liam grabbed the stranger, placed him in an arm bar, and dragged him outside. Pushing him against the wall, Liam growled in his ear. "Who the fuck are you?"

"A friend of Jaspers… I heard what happened and needed to make sure she was ok."

"Sit right here and don't move. You hear me?" Liam shoved him into the previously occupied chair and pushed back into Felicity's room. His heart nearly shattered when he saw her. She had her knees drawn up to her chest with the sheet pulled tightly around her. Tears had soaked the sheet, making it nearly transparent.

"Felicity?" Liam approached her bed. Sitting on the edge, he placed his hand on the top of her knee, causing her to jump. "Felicity, you're safe. Can you nod, letting me know you hear me?" She slowly dipped her head. "Can you tell me who that man is?"

"Where… where is he?" Her voice cracked as she spoke.

"He's outside, sitting in a chair. A friend of Jaspers?" Liam probed.

Felicity nodded, "Yes… he was," She closed her eyes. "He watched Jasper." Her swallow was audible as her body shook.

Liam instinctively reached out and pulled her to his chest, "Felicity—I won't let him hurt you." He brushed her hair flat with his hand. "What do you mean he watched Jasper?"

"When Jasper…" She took a deep breath, inhaling Liam's scent. It seemed to calm her as she slightly relaxed into his arms. "Rob was in the room."

It took Liam a moment to let the words sink in. "You mean to tell me that mother fucker was in your house when Jasper did this to you?"

Felicity stiffened against him. Liam's anger palpitated through the room. He jerked away from her and started toward the door.

Felicity pleaded with him to stop. "Liam… stop, please."

"I'll be back in a minute." Liam stepped out, leaving her in the empty room.

As soon as he stepped outside, he found Rob sitting in the chair where he'd left him. Liam moved with a ferocious speed, fisting his shirt at his neck. Lifting him from the chair, Liam pressed him against the wall.

"YOU MOTHER FUCKER!" Liam spat in his face. "You saw Jasper doing that to her and did nothing."

Several nurses and Felicity's doctor rushed to their side.

"Whoa, son, put him down."

"THIS MOTHER FUCKING BASTARD WATCHED AS JASPER RAPED HER… HE DID NOTHING," Liam bellowed out.

The doctor separated them, pulling Liam off him. Hospital security had arrived, detaining Rob while Liam paced. He pulled his phone out, calling his Lieutenant, Arden. He pushed his finger in Rob's face. "I hope you rot in jail." Spitting on his feet as he walked away.

Liam took several deep breaths, staring at Felicity's door. It hit him instantly. His dad and Hanson were right. He loved the woman sitting on the other side. He nearly came unhinged when she told him Rob was there—but more than that, holding her as he had cracked away, the remaining wall barricading his heart.

He had to talk to her.

She needed to know how he felt.

CHAPTER 19

Felicity could hear him bellowing in rage just outside her door. She had been so scared when she woke to find Rob standing at the foot of her bed, but then Liam burst in and saved her again. She felt shame when he'd pulled her close—then something else. No longer did she worry about what he thought. Instead, she was relieved to be in his arms. And that made her feel guilty. She didn't deserve his kindness after breaking his heart all those years ago.

Felicity pushed the sheet from her body and swung her legs off the bed. Grabbing her IV stand, Felicity went to a standing position. The room swirled, causing her to tilt briefly. She slowly trudged towards the bathroom, nearly getting knocked over by Liam as he pushed into her room again.

"Umpfh…" Felicity huffed out as she walked into his steel frame.

"Shit—Felicity… are you ok?" Liam gripped her arms, steadying her body. He pushed her back, checking her over as he stepped out of her way. "Why are you up?"

Felicity slid her stand between them, using it as a buffer. "I needed to use the restroom."

Liam took her elbow and guided her into the restroom. "Let me help you." He swiveled around her and helped situate her IV. "OK, I'll be outside. Holler when you're done." He darted from the tiny space, leaving Felicity standing in shock. Snapping from her confused state, she did her business, washed her hands, and stepped out. Liam was sitting on her bed, waiting. Seeing her, he jumped up and stalked toward her.

"Liam," Felicity said his name. "Stop. I can do it myself." She pushed at his hand when he tried to help her onto the bed.

"I know you can do it yourself… but Fels, you don't have to. Let me help—*please*." His eyes were filled with an emotion that scared her.

Felicity appraised the man standing before her. "Why are you here, Liam?"

Liam scooted in next to her after she got situated under the sheet. He brushed his fingers down the side of her face, which was hardly swollen. "Does it hurt?"

"Liam," she growled, grabbing his hand. "Why. Are. You. Here?"

He rubbed his face, sighing into his hand. "When I saw you tied to that bed," Felicity stiffened at his words, but Liam laid his palm on her leg. "I was so scared, Felicity. Scared you wouldn't wake up," he took a breath. "But mostly, I was scared I wouldn't be able to tell you how I felt."

Felicity sucked in a gasp, fear, shock, a myriad of emotions rushing through her. "What do you mean… how you feel? Liam, you should hate me. I was so selfish all those years ago —I've lived with regret and heartache for so long. And look at me now; that mistake has led me to become this shell of a person. I deserve where I sit."

Liam grabbed her good hand. "Don't you say that, Felicity. You don't deserve anything that asshole did to you. And yes, when you left, it hurt me deeply, but almost losing you made me realize that even though you left me hurt and angry, I still love you. I don't know what that means, but you needed to hear me say how I feel. I'm here for you—anything you need, I want to be the one to get it for you, ok?"

She was still digesting what he told her when the doctor came in, interrupting her thoughts. "Felicity," He smiled, pulling her chart from the door shelf. "I have some great news."

Peeling her stunned gaze from Liam, "What is it?"

"Your blood work looked great this morning, and you are farther along than I expected in your recovery. I'm going to have the nurse take you upstairs for some x-rays to see how the rest is healing, but if it comes back, as I suspect it will, you can go home tomorrow." He smiled. "Have you thought about where you will stay?"

"My house." Liam and Felicity spoke at the same time.

"What?" She turned to Liam. "No… absolutely not. I want to be in my house."

"Well…" The doctor chuckled. "Looks like you two need to talk. I'll leave you for now. The nurse will be by in a little while."

Liam turned to Felicity as soon as the door closed. "You should stay with me and my dad."

"No. Liam," She shifted in the bed. "I need to go home. It's important I don't let Jasper ruin my house for me, too. Plus, you don't control this."

The nurse came in, saving Felicity from his response. She was still confused over his revelation of still loving her, so she was grateful that the nurse had arrived when she did.

CHAPTER 20

Everything about being in her house made her skin crawl. But there was no way in hell she would tell Liam. She insisted she needed to be there the day she'd been released. After arguing for thirty minutes, he conceded and agreed to take her home. When she walked through the door and saw the destroyed living room, the red-stained floor, and the tattered remains of her couch, she fell to the floor in the most ungraceful manner possible and cried. Liam picked her up, carried her to her parent's room, lay her in the bed, and left to clean downstairs. He spent over an hour scrubbing the floor and removing the damaged furniture, leaving the living room empty but clean. Once he finished, he found her in the bedroom, still crying, and held her.

Then, without warning, he walked her downstairs and made her some food. Nearly three weeks later, she stared at the brand-new couch he'd bought for her.

Plus… Liam never left.

At first, he slept in the spare bedroom but moved to the floor of her parent's room when her nightmares kept waking him. Felicity told him she was fine and didn't need him to worry about her, but every time she woke screaming, he was there, patting her back and helping her get back to sleep.

"Felicity," Liam stood, dressed in his uniform, leaning against the kitchen counter. "I think you need to talk with someone. Your nightmares are getting worse, not better."

Felicity knew he was right, but she wasn't ready to discuss it. "No, I'll be fine. They'll pass."

"You won't even go into the bedroom, Felicity. Are you just going to keep the door closed forever?"

"You know, you can go home anytime, Liam. I didn't ask you to stay here." Felicity stood storming from the room and ran upstairs. She paused briefly at what was once her bedroom before slamming the door to her parents' room. Liam was right, and that pissed her off. She tried to go into that room several times while Liam was at work, but each time, she'd nearly had a panic attack.

"Felicity," Liam knocked at the door. "I'm worried about you." She heard his radio. "Shit… look, I have to leave. I'll be back tonight. Call me if you need something, and Felicity," he paused. "Think about what I said."

Felicity flopped onto the bed, her head racing with confusion. One more week, and she'd be back at work. Maybe some normalcy would help her.

When she was sure Liam had left, she grabbed her keys and headed out. She needed to talk to someone, not a therapist, but someone. She pulled into Hank Carter's driveway. He'd been like a dad to her growing up, and every time he'd visited her since getting out of the hospital, he reminded her he was only down the road if she needed something. Well, *she* needed something.

Hank had the door open before she made it out of the car. "Felicity—I hoped you'd come by." He greeted her with a hug when she got to the top of the steps.

"Yeah… I need…" her words trailed off. Hank, sensing her struggle, wrapped her in another bear hug.

"It's alright, sweet girl. Come in here and sit down. We'll talk as slow or as fast as you need."

Felicity sat on the couch, wringing her hands in her lap. "Liam wants me to go see a therapist."

"That might be the best advice that boy has ever given."

Felicity's head snapped up, pinning Hank, who sat opposite her. "Wha…what?" she asked, confused.

"Look. You went through something awful, and Liam told me about the nightmares. Felicity, shit like that doesn't just go away. You need to tell a therapist, hell, anyone really, about what happened. We can all guess based on what we saw after, but only you know. Only you lived through it. And you did."

"Did what?"

"Lived through it," Hank said matter of fact.

"Hank," Felicity shifted in her seat. "Why is Liam helping me like this? What I did to your son all those years ago—well, he shouldn't want me around at all. It's all so confusing."

"Sweet girl, you were just a kid when that all went down. You needed to see what life was like, and I don't begrudge you for your choices. While Liam carried around his misguided anger for so long, seeing you near death puts things in perspective for someone. He never stopped loving you. And I suspect you never stopped loving him. Am I right?"

"I don't know… I mean…" Felicity looked at her lap. She knew deep down no one ever amounted to Liam, "You're right. It was a decision I've regretted."

"Then you need to get some help. Otherwise, this will be a wall between you. Not because Liam is to blame or you're to blame. No… you need to get a fresh head so you can let him love you the way you deserve—and love him the way he deserves. Is that what you want?"

"What I want is to go back in time. What I want is for Liam not to have seen me tied to a bed like an animal. What I want…" Felicity paused and took a cleansing breath, "What I want is for Liam to stop looking at me as though I'm broken."

Hank moved to sit next to Felicity. He wrapped an arm around her shoulder, "Girl, that boy looks at you like you're his world—not something broken. Next time you see him staring, really look. You'll find love in his eyes, not pity."

Felicity sat with Hank for a little longer, talking about the past and things she'd missed. He reminded her that not everything was as it seemed on the surface and to look deeper. After she got home, she stopped making excuses and made an appointment with a therapist. She wanted to feel whole again, and this was the first step.

CHAPTER 21

FELICITY WAS ALL NERVES AS SHE PULLED INTO DR. BORNE'S office. She'd finally gotten the cast removed and cleared for work. Even though it was a Friday, and she would only work one day this week, she was ecstatic. She had been fortunate and wouldn't need physical therapy for her wrist—even though she'd essentially be doing PT every day when working with clients. Her eye was still a colorful shade of green, similar to an avocado, but her vision had been spared. Cutting the engine, she hurried from the car and headed inside.

"FELICITY!" Lila screamed and ran to her side, pulling her into a fierce hug.

Felicity peeled herself away from her grip. "Christ, Lila, you just saw me two days ago."

"I know… but this is different. You're back to work!"

It had been eight weeks since she'd been gone. Eight *long* weeks with Liam in her house. He refused to leave until she agreed to get therapy, which she did after talking to Hank. The nightmares stopped, but Liam was still there.

"It hasn't been that long… what's new?"

Dr. Borne appeared from a room. "Felicity!" he grabbed her for a hug. "So glad you're back! How's everything?"

"Great—everything is going… great." She laughed, "I've been seeing a counselor, and the nightmares have stopped. I still haven't gone into my room, but baby steps."

"And Liam?" Dr. Borne smirked. Everyone knew Liam was practically living with her.

Felicity sighed. "He's still there."

"You should be happy to have him there—if anything, he is nice to look at." Dr. Borne winked at her.

Lila's jaw dropped. "Dr. Borne!"

"What, I might be married to a hot firefighter, but you've got to agree he's nice to look at. And he is totally in love with you. That boy did not let up when he thought you were in danger. And Mike said he was like a raging bull on the scene."

Felicity shook her head, "Yes… I've heard it all before. Now, is my first patient here?"

"We can take a hint. Yes, they're waiting in room four." Lila sighed dramatically.

The day flew by. It felt great to be back in a semi-normal routine. Lila and Felicity locked up together and headed out to the parking lot.

Lila tilted her head at Felicity. "You feel like getting a drink?"

"You know what… I do. I couldn't have done anything like this in the past. Let's go."

They headed to a local dive and scooted up to the bar. Lila ordered them margaritas, and they chatted while they waited for the bartender to bring the drinks over.

"Alright, spill." Lila snatched the cool glass and sipped through her straw, staring at Felicity.

"Spill what?"

"Liam?" She asked in a 'well duh' kind of tone.

Felicity shrugged like it was no big deal. "There's nothing to spill. He has been practically living at my house, helping me through this. That's it."

"Seriously? Felicity… you can't tell me that boy doesn't mean something to you."

Felicity sucked the sweet liquid through the straw, the burn of the tequila making its way down her throat. "I don't know."

"Felicity…" Lila grunted.

"Fine… he means something. He's always meant something. But I'm a broken mess. He deserves better."

Lila sighed as her head shook. "You're as blind as they come. First Jasper, now Liam."

Felicity sloshed her drink, flicking the straw. "Don't you dare compare the two of them."

"I don't mean they're anything alike. You don't see what's right in front of your nose. Jasper was bad… you ignored it. Liam, though… that man looks at you like you're the only woman in the room. Did you know he cried in the hospital?"

"He didn't."

Lila arched a brow as she pinned Felicity with a serious glare. "Yes… he did. He told me he'd been so stupid and angry for so long. And that if he didn't get the chance to tell you how sorry he was, he'd regret it. Now tell me that's not love."

Felicity couldn't speak. She was trying to pretend it wasn't possible, but she'd been paying attention like Hank had told her. And she saw the same thing everyone had been telling her. Liam looked at her like he loved her. She couldn't accept it—even though he'd said it to her face.

"I need another one." Felicity drank down another margarita, the effects of the alcohol hitting her quicker than she expected. Lila was also buzzed and offered to call her a cab, but she called Liam. She knew he'd come pick her up, no questions asked. And when he picked up on the first ring, he did exactly what she thought he would do. He told her to sit tight and that he would be there in a few minutes.

CHAPTER 22

Felicity watched as Liam opened her front door and walked inside. She followed him, tossing her bag on the entry table.

"Felicity, I know you were just having a good time, but you need to be more careful."

"Liam—I am a grown woman who wanted to drink with a friend. Calm down. I didn't drive. I called you. Jesus." She flopped onto the couch.

He watched her, sitting in the space beside her, "I know. Sorry, I love you, ok? I don't want to see you get hurt."

Felicity appraised the man in front of her. Everything everyone had been telling her had just come out of his mouth —again. "How can you love me?"

"WHAT?" He barked out, "What kind of question is that?"

"A serious one. I'm not the woman you knew back in high school. I'm broken and tarnished. Someone ruined me. You deserve someone who will protect your heart, not rip it to pieces like I did."

"You're not ruined. And there hasn't been another woman since you that I've even come close to loving. It's always been you. The moment I thought I was going to lose you… I knew the anger I held onto was stupid. Here you were, back in town—it was like God was telling me it was our chance again. Felicity, I'll be here when you're ready to let me in again. I love you, and that will not change."

She couldn't breathe. Here was the only boy… now the man she'd ever really loved—and he told her he still loved her. She reached out, pressing her hand to his face. "Thank you, Liam."

Liam could only stare at Felicity. He wanted to reach out and pull her to him, but he knew it was too soon. It had only been two months since she'd been brutalized and tortured. She was doing well on the surface, but he knew the demons she held inside. He was here at night when she woke screaming.

"You're welcome. Now… let's get you to bed. It's late, and you're technically still recovering."

Liam helped her from the couch and followed her upstairs. She was slightly wobbly on her feet, so he stayed close behind her as they ascended the steps. Felicity paused briefly, staring at the door to her room, which she had yet to enter. Shaking the memory from her head, she continued to the master bedroom.

Liam sat on the edge of the bed, watching Felicity as she tried to decide what to do. "What's wrong? You look lost."

"I think I want to shower." She smiled, grabbed some clothes from the dresser, and disappeared into the bathroom.

Liam stripped to his boxers and slipped beneath the sleeping bag on the floor. He'd taken to sleeping on the floor after the first week of staying here. Since Felicity had refused to stay at his house with him and his dad, he'd refused to leave. And he was glad he'd fought her on it. She'd woken up almost every night since with nightmares. Usually, she never fully woke up. Some nights, he'd have to sit beside her, holding her hand until she fell asleep. Liam was exhausted, but until the nightmares stopped, he'd fight through his tiredness and help her.

He'd just closed his eyes when the bathroom door opened, and Felicity emerged. She was wearing a pair of tiny shorts and a tight tank top. Liam had to adjust himself, reminding his cock she wasn't ready. Felicity yawned, stretching her arms overhead, teasing him with a sliver of her flesh, before crawling into bed.

"You know, you can go sleep in the other room. I don't need you to stay in here."

"Yeah—well, unless your nightmares have magically disappeared, this is the best way for me to get some kind of sleep."

Felicity let out a growl. "Fine."

She flicked the light off, casting the room into darkness, and closed her eyes.

CHAPTER 23

Liam woke to her screams—like clockwork. Felicity would writhe and cry out into the dark room. He lay there, waiting to see if she would go back to sleep.

"No…No…Please—don't. JASPER!" She screamed out, bolting upright in the bed. Liam jumped from the floor and sat down on the edge of the bed.

"Felicity," he whispered, trying to assess if she was awake or still stuck inside her terror. Her sobs broke his heart. He wanted nothing more than to reach inside her head and banish the things that tormented her. "Felicity, please wake up." He gently clasped her shoulder. She flopped back onto the bed, her sobs louder than when she was crying out.

"I hate this." She cried into her pillow, "I'm so broken."

Liam wiped her hair from her face. "You're not broken. You went through something awful, and it will get better in time." He pulled the covers back up, tucking them in around her. "Try to get some sleep." As he slid back to the floor, she called out.

"Liam. Will you just lay next to me for a little while? Maybe until I fall back asleep?"

He squeezed his eyes shut. She wanted him to hold her, and even if this wasn't how he wanted it to be, he stood and slipped in beside her. "Alright, close your eyes. I'll stay here until you fall back asleep."

Liam stared at the ceiling, listening as Felicity's breathing evened out. He was relieved to hear her relax some. Closing his eyes, he gave her a few more minutes before slipping out of bed and returning to the floor.

THE GLOW of the sunlight warmed Felicity's face, stirring her from her restless sleep. Opening her eyes, she realized she was cocooned in the human blanket, Liam. His leg was slung over hers, and his arm held her close to his chest. She couldn't help but notice that even though he was snoring, part of him was wide awake. She ground her behind against him, sparking a moan from behind her. Liam pressed into her, then realizing what he was doing, jerked, causing himself to roll onto the floor.

"Shit."

Felicity couldn't contain her giggle. "Oh my god, are you alright?"

He rubbed his head. "I should ask you that. I meant to get back on the floor last night, but apparently, my body enjoyed your mattress a little too much."

Felicity's eyes flicked to the tent in his boxers, and she smiled. "I think your body enjoyed more than my mattress."

Liam covered his very prominent erection with his hands. "Felicity, I… god, this is embarrassing."

"Why are you embarrassed? It's not like I don't know what it looks like."

Liam shrugged as he squeezed his eyes closed. "Well, yeah. But it's inconsiderate of me. You're not ready for this yet. I should have been more careful."

Felicity slid out from under the covers and crawled across the bed. She propped herself on her knees and smiled at Liam. "Liam." She held out her hand, beckoning him closer. He took it, allowing her to pull him towards her. "You have nothing to apologize for. And more careful? Careful of what?"

"I just don't want you to think…" his words died.

"Sex? You're worried. I think you want sex?"

He nodded as his skin flushed with embarrassment.

"I don't think that. In fact," she tugged him closer. "You have treated me like glass for far too long. I'm not ready for that…" she shuddered. "But you told me you loved me and have not even attempted to kiss me. Why?"

Liam stood there, frozen. He did not know why he hadn't tried to kiss her. He just knew he worried about messing up her healing, inside and outside. Figuring she'd let him know when she was ready for anything, he realized, staring down at her now, that he'd been wrong.

"Well?" She probed again.

Liam didn't think. He just pressed his lips to hers. She froze at first, and Liam feared he'd made a mistake. But she wound her fingers into his hair and pulled him in closer. Their bodies pressed into one another, and the kiss turned fierce. It was everything he'd remembered. Her moist lips moved with his in sync. Her tongue danced with his. Her soft moans made his cock jump in anticipation.

Breaking the kiss, Liam rested his forehead on hers. "I missed that—no… I missed us." He kissed her face, stepping away from her hold. "But if I don't go shower, my dick will override my brain. And you are definitely not ready for that."

CHAPTER 24

Felicity's life had fallen into a semi-normal routine. Liam had moved in with her since she was still afraid of being alone. He'd moved from the floor, too, sharing her bed in a very platonic way. Her visits with her therapist had helped decrease her nightmares, but they still interrupted her week. As she sat in the living room watching T.V., waiting for Liam to get home, her mind wandered. She climbed the steps towards her bedroom. Before she knew it, she was standing outside her bedroom door. Felicity had yet to enter as she'd steered clear of the reminders held behind the wooden barrier that protected her from the hell she so longed to bury.

Placing her hand on the cool brass knob, she took a deep breath and twisted. Closing her eyes as she stepped inside, she took several deep breaths. The words of her therapist on repeat in her head, *"The room is just a room. Nothing more."*

Peeling her eyes open, her breath caught in her throat. The room was just as she expected it to be, broken—just like her. Her lungs burned as she tried to catch her breath. Her vision swam, spots of red flashing in her mind. Dropping to her knees, she couldn't control the sobs as they spilled from her lips.

Arms wrapped around her, "I got you, Felicity."

Liam. He had her. Felicity went as he tugged her into his lap. His warm embrace shielded her as she gave in to the overdue need to mourn her loss.

Her loss of the life she'd once had. Losing her mother. Losing her dignity and losing herself.

Liam held her on the floor of her bedroom for what felt like an eternity. When the tears dried up, she wiped her face and snorted.

"Feel better?"

Shrugging her shoulders, she burrowed her face into his chest. "I don't know how to feel."

"Ok." Liam squeezed her tighter.

"When will this go away? Am I always going to be broken, Liam?"

"Felicity," He shifted to look into her eyes, "You're not broken. Stop saying that."

"Liam…" she pulled out of his arms and pushed up to stand. Pacing the floor, "You deserve a woman who can give you what you need."

Liam jumped to his feet. "Felicity… what is it you think I need?"

"A woman who can love you how you should be loved."

"Is this about sex?" Liam asked.

Felicity bristled, "Well… yeah—that too. But you don't get sleep because you're dealing with my nightmares. I can't even go into my room, Liam."

"Felicity."

She paced the room, pulling at her hair.

"FELICITY," Liam said her name louder, causing her to jump.

"WHAT?"

"Look around. You're in your room. You've avoided the door for three months like it would bite you. Now… here you are, having a conversation with me. In. Your. Room."

Felicity looked around, realizing he was right… and she wasn't having a panic attack. She sat on the bed, her hands feeling the fluffy comforter. Glancing over her shoulder, she stared at the headboard. Flashbacks to the days she spent as Jasper's captive skittered across her mind—yet the panic she expected to feel didn't come. Instead, anger filled her veins. Standing, she fisted the material and pulled. Stripping the bed completely. Pillow and sheets fluttered to the floor. Liam watched as she tore through the linens. She ripped the pillows, feathers dusting the surrounding room. Screaming, she flung the tattered remains across the room, smacking Liam in the chest. She froze, realizing what she'd done.

"Oh, my God. I'm sorry." Her voice wavering as she watched for his reaction.

Liam picked up the partially shredded fabric, toying with it between his fingers. He smiled at Felicity before shaking it furiously at her, spilling the remaining feathers into the air.

White down filtered the air, latching onto her hair. Felicity stood wide-eyed before erupting into a fit of giggles.

"What?" Liam plucked a feather from his lips.

"Look at this mess." Felicity spun, pointing to the room now covered in a blanket of white. "It looks like a duck died in here."

Liam walked behind her, pulling her against his chest. "You're not broken. I don't need anyone else. I love you, Felicity. And I will tell you every day until you believe me."

"But you deserve so much more."

"I'll take what I can from you… and wait as long as I have to for more." He squeezed her against him.

CHAPTER 25

It'd been six months since her life had been irrevocably changed. Her nightmares were almost non-existent now. Some of that involved Liam staying with her through it all. They'd somehow found their friendship amid her hell, but Felicity wanted more. Liam had been nothing but patient with her. A few kisses were shared, but that was it—and it was driving her nuts.

"So, you still going to surprise him?" Lila asked as she bit into her donut. She'd been helping Felicity plan the surprise for the last few days.

Felicity grinned. "Yes. I think it's time."

"You sure you're ready?"

She turned toward her friend. "I think so. My therapist said I need to just go slow, but damn… he won't even touch me beyond a hug or a kiss. I want more, Lila."

"I know. But you need to be sure… and be prepared for it not to go the way you want." Lila smiled at her.

"Yeah… I know. I need to feel…" She took a breath. "*Human*."

Lila shrugged before walking out of the break room. Felicity knew she was right—this could all explode in her face. But she needed to try. She needed to see if she could be a real woman and give herself to the man she loved.

FELICITY RUSHED home when she finished for the day. She wanted to beat Liam home so she could surprise him. She practically ran up the stairs and tore her clothes off. After primping, she slipped on her heels and went downstairs to wait.

"Felicity?" Liam called out from the front door.

"In here," she called out, her skin prickling with nerves as she waited to see his reaction.

"What the fuck?" Liam's eyes widened as Arden rammed into his back, and he froze. Felicity stood in the kitchen wearing nothing but a red lace bra and a matching red thong—well, that and a pair of come fuck me heels.

"Oh my God." Felicity tried to cover herself, folding her arms across her chest.

Liam spun, shoving Arden back out the way they came. Felicity heard the door slam shut, leaving her alone and completely embarrassed. Plopping into the chair, she pressed her hands to her face, trying to banish the tears building.

"Felicity," Liam pulled the chair beside her, "I'm so sorry. I didn't know you'd be…"

"Nearly naked?" she peeked through her fingers.

"Yeah… that."

She blew out a breath. "God, I'm so stupid."

"Stupid is not the word that comes to mind. Sexy… mouth-watering… hot, maybe—but not stupid. Was this for me?" Liam pulled her hand from her face, lacing his fingers with hers as he stood beside her.

"Yeah… I wanted to surprise you."

"You did…" he eyed her luscious curves as he paused. "Surprise me. Arden, too—I think he might be in complete shock." Liam laughed.

Felicity covered her face with her other hand. "How embarrassing. I won't be able to look him in the face again."

"You should not be embarrassed. Come here," He tugged her hand, encouraging her to stand. "Let me see you."

Felicity stood up, giving him a perfect view. Liam ran his hand down her smooth skin. "You. Are. Beautiful."

Goosebumps prickled her skin, "Liam." His name was breathless against her lips.

"Is this ok?" He asked as he continued tracing her skin with his fingertips, never breaking eye contact.

"Mmmhum." She mumbled.

Liam continued his slow exploration of her body. He watched her as his fingers moved across her stomach, then up across her lace-covered breasts. Felicity's breath hitched as he slowly thumbed her pert nipple, pressing against the fabric. Liam wound his fingers into her hair as he pulled her in for a kiss. As soon as their lips met, Felicity's whole body felt as though it was on fire.

"Liam," she broke free, "I… I…"

"What do you want, Felicity?"

She ducked her head. "I want you."

"Look at me, Felicity. I need to see your eyes when you say it."

She tilted her head up. "I want you, please."

"If we do this," he pulled her chin up. "You need to understand you're in control. At any time you feel uncomfortable, you tell me to stop." She froze, not knowing what to say. "I need you to nod or say something. Or this isn't happening."

Slowly, Felicity nodded as she whispered her response. "Ok."

Liam smashed his lips to hers, his tongue tangling with hers, and her body melded against his. A moan escaped from her as she ground her hips into him. "Not here." Liam tugged her hand, herding her towards the stairs.

"Wait." Felicity paused, glancing at the stairwell. "I don't want to go upstairs."

Liam glanced over his shoulder, then back to her. Nodding, he changed direction and moved them towards the couch. Laying her down, he kneeled over her and brushed her hair from her face. "Remember, you're in control."

Nodding, Felicity ran her hand down his face, cupping his cheek. "I'm in control."

CHAPTER 26

Every part of her was on fire. Her body was reacting to every single touch as Liam explored her. His knee was wedged between her legs, holding him in place above her as he kissed her. A trail of flames followed his lips as he moved down her neck into the hollow of her shoulder. As Liam traced his hand down her side, Felicity hissed and bucked her hips into him. She could feel his arousal pressing against his jeans. Her hands pulled at his belt, begging him without words.

"Not yet," Liam mumbled against her mouth as he tugged her hands into his. He pushed her hands above her head, licking her nipple through the lace material. Felicity moaned as he dipped his tongue beneath the edge. Liam pinned her hands to the couch as he nibbled her pink flesh.

Felicity sucked in a breath. Flashes of Jasper pinning her down assaulted her memory, causing her to squeeze her eyes closed. Her body must have gone stiff because Liam paused, lifting his head.

"Felicity… you still with me?" She kept her eyes closed, nodding as she willed the memory gone. "No, baby. Open your eyes. I need to know this is ok."

"Please, keep going."

Liam released her hands and pushed himself off her body. "Felicity, talk to me."

She sat up, drawing her legs to her chest, and buried her head into her knees. Tears spilled down her thighs. "Why can't I be normal? I'm so fucking broken."

Liam ran his hand up her shin. "You're not broken. It's just too soon. I should have known better."

Anger filled her chest, "WHAT? I did this. I wanted to feel normal, Liam. This isn't on you. You should go." Felicity stood.

"What? Felicity, you're not making sense."

"I want you to leave, Liam. You should be with someone who isn't a fucked-up mess."

Liam stood, tugging her into his chest. He wrapped his arms around Felicity. "I'm not going anywhere. Sex isn't the only thing a relationship is made of, Fels. And I told you I'd wait as long as I needed to for you to be ready."

Her eyes welled with more tears. "What if I'm never ready?"

"You will be. Stop trying to rush this." Liam brushed his fingers through her hair.

Her face morphed into one filled with anger. "I didn't rush this. Please… I want to feel human. Do you understand?"

"So, you want to use me to feel human?" Liam pulled back, looking down at her in his arms.

"No…" Felicity shook her head, "Well… yeah, I guess it sounds like that, but no—I want to be with the man I love."

"What did you just say?" Liam couldn't believe his ears. He'd been waiting to hear her utter those words for the last few months.

"I love you, Liam. I do. And you shouldn't have to keep waiting for me to be…"

Liam cut her off as he pressed his lips to hers. He kissed her with so much passion that she was breathless when he broke apart. "You love me?"

"Yes… I do."

He smiled as he spun her around and plopped onto the couch. Sitting with his legs spread, he pulled her to stand between his knees.

"What are you doing?"

"Letting the woman who loves me use me." He quirked an eyebrow at her.

"I don't understand." Felicity ran her hands through her hair as she looked down at him.

"Baby… you just told me you love me. You can use me however you need. And I think you need to be in control. So, use me. I'm yours." He spread his arms out wide, his eyes flicking to the spot between his legs.

Felicity stared down at the selfless man on her couch. She watched in awe as he tugged his shirt over his head and unbuttoned his jeans. He never broke eye contact as he slid the denim down his legs and sat only in his black boxer briefs. He slung his arms back over the back of the couch and waited.

"You're in control."

Felicity froze. Liam looked calm as he sat with his arms draped loosely beside him. His feet were spread, allowing her to stand between his knees.

"Liam," Felicity breathed out his name.

"Felicity, I'm not moving unless you ask."

"But how…" she shook her head, "I don't understand how this will work if you don't touch me."

"Baby, my dick doesn't need my hands to take part. It needs you."

"But don't you want to touch me—I mean, don't you need to touch me too?"

He gave Felicity a heated look as he spoke. "Don't get me wrong… not touching you is going to be a challenge, but you can see I don't have to put my hands on you to get hard."

Felicity glanced down, noting the outline of his cock through the silky material. Smiling, she realized he wanted her, and he was letting her lead the encounter.

"I won't touch you unless you ask me to. Do you understand?"

"Yes." Felicity kneeled in front of him, her hands finding their way to the rugged plains of his abdomen.

The ridges of his muscles flexed and jumped as she ran her fingers across the tanned skin. His breath hitched, and he let out a hiss. Felicity watched as he gritted his teeth and squeezed his eyes shut.

She continued her exploration of his body, tracing the definition of his well-tuned physique. She slowly climbed up, straddling his lap, and pressed her lips to his. She could feel the hardness of his excitement between her legs as she ground into him. He groaned, leaning his head back onto the couch. Felicity watched him clench his hands, fighting the urge to touch her. She smiled as she pressed her mouth against his chest. Her tongue swirled around his nipple. He couldn't help it as he thrust his hips into her, moaning as he bit his lip.

Felicity ground against him, the ridge of his cock rubbing against the fabric of her panties. She slowly eased her hand lower, adjusting her legs so she could slip her hand beneath the waistband of his boxers. Liam groaned, gripping the fabric of the couch beneath his fingers. His hips came off the cushion slightly as she wrapped her fingers around his thick member. Felicity felt empowered as she stroked him. She watched his face, ecstasy written all over his tight expression. She couldn't sedate the fire burning between her legs. She needed more. Freeing his dick from the fabric, she sucked her lip into her mouth. She wanted to feel him inside her. Slowly, she rose to her knees, her hand wrapped around the base of his cock. Her eyes never strayed from his face as she pulled her panties to the side and eased him inside. Liam's eyes popped open, locking onto hers as she sheathed him fully inside her.

He dared not move, "Felicity." He breathed out, watching her as she adjusted to his size. His fist gripped the soft material as he held his body frozen. His cock pulsated like a drum inside her channel as he waited patiently for her to make the next move.

Felicity leaned back, her eyes closed as she rocked against him. Her hands pressed into his chest, and her slick cunt squeezed his cock. Liam couldn't stop watching her. He fought to keep his hands still, afraid touching her would break the spell she'd weaved around them. Her head rolled forward, and her eyes met his.

"Touch me," she whispered. She slid her hand up his chest, across his shoulder, taking his hand in hers. She pulled it down, pressing his palm against her hip. "Please, Liam. I need you to touch me."

Releasing the cushion he'd been holding in a death grip, he slipped his hand to her other hip. Felicity began rocking against him. Her movements became more demanding and more frantic. Liam only held her hips, relishing in the sensation of her channel clenching him deep inside her. He knew he wouldn't last long, not with the heat of her pussy wrapped around him like she was. He could feel her muscles tighten, her breathing more like a pant.

"Oh…" she moaned, bucking harder. Their skin slapping echoed into the living room. "Liam… I think I'm going to come." She let out a squeal, her walls clamping down on his dick so hard he swore he saw stars. She moved fast, sucking his seed from him like her life depended on it.

"Felicity…" he said her name, watching her face as her orgasm washed over them. Her body slowed as she leaned forward and pressed her head to his shoulder. No words were spoken. Liam held her against him. Her soft whimpers made him realize she was crying.

"Baby? Did I hurt you—why are you crying?"

Felicity shook her head against him, "I'm not broken…" Liam wrapped his arms around her, holding her against him as she let the tears fall.

Felicity wasn't sure how long Liam had held her as she sat straddling his lap, his semi-hard cock still buried inside her. He ran his hand down her hair, pressing light kisses to her forehead.

"You ready to go to bed?" He breathed against her ear as he spoke.

"Yeah," Felicity moved to climb off his lap, but Liam gripped her tight and held onto her as he stood. His dick slipped from her, their combined juices leaking down his thighs. He carefully kicked his boxers the rest of the way off and carried her to their bedroom. Pulling back the covers, he laid her down and climbed in behind her. Wrapping an arm around her waist, he dragged her against his chest.

"I love you, Felicity." He kissed her neck.

Something clicked inside her. This man had allowed her to control sex. And damn, it felt good. Felicity rolled to face him. "I love you, too. Thank you for letting me… well, you know."

"Molest me?" Liam smiled, half laughing.

Felicity leaned into him, pressing a kiss to his mouth. She slipped her tongue past his lips, tangling it with his.

"What are you doing, Felicity?" Liam mumbled against her mouth.

"I realized something." She whispered into the room. "You're not Jasper, and I feel safe with you… you gave me something I thought I'd never get back."

Liam kissed her cheek. "I love you."

Felicity snuggled into his arms, his warmth wrapping around her. Liam rested his head against hers as his eyes closed. Everything about this woman made his heart soar.

CHAPTER 27

Almost a month passed since Liam and Felicity had been intimate… and Liam was losing his mind. He sat on the bench in the locker room, staring at the metal door. He didn't hear anyone come in, so when Chase said his name, he nearly fell off the wooden seat.

"Damn, Liam—you ok?"

Liam righted himself. "Yeah—I was lost in thought. You scared the shit out of me."

"Must have been some serious thinking to have you oblivious to my loud ass."

Liam ran his palm across his face. "Yeah."

"Whoa," Chase sat beside him, "What's wrong? This isn't like you."

"Just confused. I'll be alright." Liam stood, grabbing his duffle bag.

Chase eyed his friend. "Is it Felicity?"

Blinking, "Yeah—I just… I don't know. I thought everything was going well, but then we…" Liam paused.

"You what?"

"She wanted to feel human—her words. So, I let her have control."

"Control with what? You're not making any sense, dude."

Liam took a breath and blew it out. "Sex, Chase. We had sex."

"Oh…" Chase paused. "Oh, shit."

"Yeah. Now, she is avoiding me like the plague. I fucked up. She wasn't ready."

"Have you talked to her?"

He shrugged his shoulders and nodded. "Every time I try, she blows me off. Saying she's just busy at work."

"Maybe she is busy." Chase pointed out.

"Nah—I can sense something else. Something she's not telling me."

Chase shrugged his shoulders. "I don't know. It would be best if you talked to Arden—he's the married one. Maybe he can help."

"True, but I think I'll talk to my dad. She's close to him now… perhaps she's said something to him."

Liam patted Chase on the back as he walked out. He hoped his dad could shed some light on the matter. Because right now, it felt like she was pulling away. Liam didn't know if he could survive losing her again. The drive to his house, rather than the house he'd shared with his dad before Felicity came back into his life, seemed to take forever. He was relieved to see his dad was home.

"Dad?" He called out as he walked inside.

"Son?" His dad appeared from the kitchen. "Whatcha doing here?"

Liam stared at his dad, the emotions he held inside spilling from him like a raging bull, causing his dad to move toward him. "Liam," His dad hugged him, "What's happened? Is it Felicity? Is she alright?"

"She's fine, I think."

"Come on, sit down." His dad guided him to the couch. "Talk to me. What's got you so upset?"

Liam wiped the tears from his face. "I messed up, Dad."

"What do you mean, you messed up?"

"Um..." Liam took a breath, "Felicity and I... well," he shifted nervously in his seat.

"Sex?" His dad asked.

Liam's head popped up, "How..."

His dad cut him off. "Son, you always got nervous when you talked about sex. Am I right?"

"Yes—she wanted to feel normal. I knew she wasn't ready, but she pushed, and I gave in. But I let her be in control—and it was amazing. But now... she won't talk to me."

"Give her time."

"TIME? Dad, it's been almost a month. She avoids me like the plague. I told her then I didn't need sex and I'd wait until she was ready. She wanted this. Now she acts like—hell, I don't know."

His dad sat silently for a minute. "Have you pushed the conversation?"

"I'm afraid to push it. Dad, I can't go through losing her again. It'll break me this time."

"You're assuming the worst without talking to her?"

Liam's eyes narrowed on his father. "Has she said anything to you?"

"You should talk to her." His dad gave him a pointed look.

"Wait, she has said something to you. Tell me, Dad. Please."

He sighed. "Liam, you need to talk to her. I don't want to break her trust."

"HER TRUST. What about mine?" Liam stood, pacing the floor. "I'm. *Your*. Son."

"Liam, calm down. Christ," his dad slapped the chair arm, "She thinks you don't want her."

"WHAT?" Liam spun, pinning his dad with a glare. "What do you mean?"

"She came to me a few days ago. She was worried she'd messed everything up by forcing you to have sex with her. She thinks you're avoiding her."

"OH MY GOD. Are you fucking serious?" Liam bellowed into the room.

"Liam, she has been through something awful. Felicity is trying to find a normal balance now that part of her has been robbed—she doesn't know who she is. And even though you gave her something by allowing her to have control… she worries it will be the only way she can ever feel intimacy. She thinks you see her as glass, and she'll break. Does that make sense?"

Liam realized he was hurting her more by keeping her at a distance. Well, he knew right then he needed to change that. "Yeah—It does. Thanks, Dad. I need to go."

"Liam," his dad stood. "Fight for her. She needs you as much as you need her."

Liam nodded, rushing from the house. He was about to show Felicity how much he wanted her. He knew it might send her in a downward tailspin, but he didn't care.

It was time to stop treating her like a fragile doll.

CHAPTER 28

Felicity stood at the counter, listening to Lila complain about a patient as they closed up for the day. Her mind was not focused. She couldn't stop thinking about Liam and how he seemed so distant. It was her fault—she'd pushed him to have sex a few weeks ago.

"Are you listening to me?" Lila interrupted her train of thought.

"Yeah—no." She shrugged. "I have a lot on my mind."

"You're still worried about Liam?"

Felicity tapped her fingers on the counter. "Yeah—I think I fucked up pushing him."

Lila rolled her eyes. "I think you are overreacting. You should talk to him."

"He's avoiding me." She shrugged.

"You sure you're not the one avoiding him? I'm just saying— I know how you are."

"What does that mean?"

She shrugged her shoulders at Felicity. "You tend to get quiet and avoid the hard stuff. Think about how long it took to get you to talk to a therapist after Jasper."

Felicity winced. Lila was right—she found avoiding the issue easier than facing it head-on. "Yeah… ok. Maybe it is me. I'll try to talk to him tonight."

"Um—don't think that's going to work." Lila smiled.

"Why not?"

Her smirk grew wider. "Because he's standing behind you."

Felicity turned to see Liam standing in the doorway, and he looked pissed. "Liam? What are you doing here?"

Liam didn't answer. Instead, he took two steps toward her and pressed his lips to hers. His fingers wound into her hair, the pressure of his mouth on hers causing her to melt.

"Well—I'd say he's not distant now." Lila laughed. "Liam, the break room is empty if you need to chat. Felicity, I'll lock up on my way out."

Liam pulled away, grabbing Felicity and tossing her over his shoulder. "Thanks." He stormed down the hallway, pushed into the small break room, and slammed the door with his foot. He slid Felicity off his shoulder and sat her on the table in the center of the room.

"Liam…" He pressed his finger to her lips, silencing her words. Reaching behind him, he locked the door.

"I. Love. You." He smashed his mouth to hers again, wedging himself between her thighs.

Felicity couldn't stop the moan that bubbled up from her chest. "Liam, what's going on?"

He peppered kisses down her neck, licking and biting her ear. "You. Are. Mine." He jerked her top over her head, unclasping her bra to free her breasts. She covered herself, but Liam grabbed her arms and pinned them down. "No… let me see you."

"Liam… what if Lila hears?"

"I," he sucked her nipple into his mouth, "don't," he mumbled against her flesh, "care." He released her hand, running his palm along her side, down to her hip. His hand slipped into her scrubs, finding her hot and wet when he dipped his finger into her channel. "You're wet for me."

"Yes." She breathed out, her hand gripping the edge of the table.

"I'm going to make you come, Felicity. This time," he sucked her nipple into his mouth again, swirling his tongue around the pert flesh. It made a popping sound when he released it. "I'm in control."

She nodded, unable to find the words to respond. He pushed her back, forcing her to lie down against the cool wooden surface. "I won't hurt you." He pulled her pants off, taking her panties with them. "God, You. Are. Beautiful." He ran his fingers up her legs, the touch causing a shiver to trickle through her veins.

"Liam…" she moaned, wanting to feel him. She reached out and grabbed his arm.

"What do you want, baby?"

"You… I want you." She panted out, her chest heaving with her desire.

Liam unzipped his pants, tugging his hard cock free. His hand fisted the angry red flesh. "I'm going to fuck you so hard that anyone within a ten-mile radius is going to hear you begging me for more. Are you ready?"

Felicity expected fear, but she was bursting with need. "Yes…" she pleaded, needing him to take her hard.

Liam stepped closer. The head of his cock beaded with pre-cum, and he jacked himself. He rubbed the tip against her glistening pink folds, dripping with honey. He pushed inside a little, his fingers digging into her cunt, pulling the flesh apart so he could see himself as he buried his cock inside. Felicity flinched, her legs tightening, as she squeezed her eyes shut. She expected the visions of Jasper to take over, but then she heard Liam's voice.

"Let me inside, baby. Let me love you."

It was like a heavy weight had been lifted. She opened her eyes to see him standing between her thighs, waiting. He'd stopped, giving her the chance to say no to this. Relaxing her body, she spread her legs and wrapped them around him.

"I'm yours." She breathed out, beckoning him inside. Liam smiled, then pushed himself into her channel. His cock filled her completely. This time, it was different. She wasn't in control, yet she didn't feel afraid. Liam leaned down, covering her body with his as his lips found hers. As he moved, their tongues tangled, skin upon skin, as he dove into the depths of her.

She could feel something building, "Oh god, Liam… I—" Her body tensed.

"Let go, Felicity. I'll be here to catch you." His hips pounded into her, his dick sliding effortlessly between her folds. His orgasm building, "I can't last long. Your pussy feels too good, baby. Come for me."

Felicity let go, and her cunt clenched his cock so hard she nearly blacked out from the orgasm as it ripped through her veins. Every single nerve was on fire as she called out his name. Liam jerked, his come filling her womb as he toppled over the cliff with her.

Their pants were the only sound that filled the tiny space. "Shit… I know Lila heard us if she's still here." Liam laughed.

"Liam?" Felicity pushed up on her elbows, Liam's semi-hard cock still buried inside her.

He wiped the sweat covering his brow. "Yeah?"

"What the hell just happened?"

He laughed, "I needed to show you are whole, baby. And that I don't see you as glass. But mostly that I'm not him."

"Oh God—Liam," Felicity sat up, shifting against him, "You could never be him. I love you." She wiggled against his growing erection.

"Fels, while I enjoyed every second of what we just did. You need to stop before I have to fuck you again. And I'd like to take you home first."

She chuckled, pressing a kiss to his chest. "Maybe I want to go home in a few." She tugged him closer by wrapping her legs around his ass, pulling his dick deeper. "You fixed me. I don't see Jasper anymore. And we have some catching up to do."

Felicity threw her arms around his neck, pulling herself up to drape around him. She shifted, grinding her pussy against his pelvic bone. "OH…" she moaned, tilting her head back.

"Damn, woman. You're going to kill me." Liam lifted Felicity and pressed her against the door, "I. Love. You."

Felicity smiled, pressing her lips against his, "I love you too… now… fuck me so we can go home."

Liam did just that. He fucked the love of his life against the break room door. She came around his cock like a waterfall, causing him to fill her up again. Once they got cleaned up, he followed her home.

"Let's get married." Liam blurted out as they walked inside together.

"What…" Felicity spun to look at Liam, "What did you say?"

"I said… Let's get married."

She held his gaze. "Are you asking me to marry you?"

Liam stepped towards her, slipping his hand in hers, and kneeled. "Felicity…" He looked into her eyes. "When you left me all those years ago, I never got over you. Then—when I almost lost you again… I swore I'd do anything to make you mine for good. You had my heart then… you have my heart now. It belongs to you, and yours belongs to me. Protect my heart, and let me protect yours… Marry me?"

"Yes…" Felicity dropped to her knees, "Yes… I'll marry you."

Liam pulled her into his arms. "I love you, Felicity."

CHAPTER 29

They'd married in a small ceremony at the justice of the peace a few months after he'd asked her. Lila and his dad were the only people there. Felicity said she didn't want anything big because her mom wasn't there to walk her down the aisle. Liam didn't care. He just wanted to marry her. Felicity still saw her therapist, but with Liam's help, she buried the memories of what happened in the past. Plus, sex with Liam was so far from what it had been with Jasper that she couldn't get enough.

Now, a year later, they were celebrating their anniversary. Liam had made dinner reservations at a local pub at Felicity's request. She hadn't been feeling well and didn't want to chance getting sick in a fancy restaurant.

"So, you going to dinner tonight?" Lila asked as they closed the office.

Felicity answered but was blindsided by an overwhelming urge to vomit. She darted by Lila, barely reaching the toilet before she lost her lunch.

"Holy shit, Felicity. You, ok?"

Felicity looked up from the toilet. "I haven't been feeling great. Fuck… I guess I'm ruining dinner—I must have a bug."

"Or you're pregnant." Lila joked.

Felicity looked at her friend with a panicked glare, "Oh. Shit."

"I was kidding, kind of. Felicity—when was your last period?"

"Um… I don't know. I think…" Felicity rested her head on the toilet, "Fuck."

"Let me run and grab a test." Lila disappeared, returning a few minutes later with a pregnancy test. "Get up. You need to pee on this."

She ripped open the test and stared at the stick. "What am I going to do? I can't be pregnant."

Lila leaned against the door and watched her. "Why not? Does Liam not want kids?"

"I don't know. We never talked about it before."

"Well… pee on that. Until you know, no sense in freaking out."

Felicity flushed the toilet before standing and ripping the box open. "I can't pee if you're staring at me."

Lila turned around. "I ain't leaving."

Felicity shook her head and pushed her scrubs down. She couldn't be pregnant, could she?

The next few minutes were the longest in her life. "I can't look."

Lila grabbed the stick. "Oh. My. God."

Felicity yanked the plastic wand from her hands.

Pregnant.

"FELICITY, YOU OK?" Liam studied his wife. "You've been so quiet. We didn't have to come out if you aren't feeling well. I'd have been just as happy at the house with you."

"No… I'm fine." She shifted in her seat.

Liam set down his fork. "Fels… it's me you're talking to. You're not fine. Out with it. What's the matter?"

Felicity stared at the man in front of her. She loved him with everything she was, and he loved her just as fiercely. Hopefully, this wouldn't change that.

"Um… well," Felicity took a sip of her water, "It looks like we're going to have a baby."

Liam shrugged, "That's all? Wait…" his head snapped. "Did you say a baby?"

"Yeah—I'm pregnant."

Liam stood so quickly that his chair toppled backward, clattering to the floor. The restaurant got eerily quiet as they watched him move around the table toward her.

"I'M GOING TO BE A DAD!" He pumped his fist into the air, causing the restaurant to erupt in cheers while clapping their hands.

"Are you sure?" He squatted next to Felicity, placing his hand on her abdomen.

"Pretty sure. I took a test before I came home." She took a calming breath. "I'll see my doctor for some bloodwork tomorrow and an ultrasound to confirm. You're happy about this?" Felicity questioned Liam.

"Oh, baby… this is the best news ever." He hugged her ferociously, squeezing the air from her lungs.

"Liam…" She gasped at the force of his embrace.

"Shit—Sorry, baby. Did I hurt you?" He let go, appraising her body like he'd hurt her or the baby.

Felicity cupped his cheek. "I'm fine. So, you're happy, not mad?"

"Why would I be mad?" His brows furrowed in confusion.

"We didn't exactly plan this, Liam. I wasn't sure how you would feel."

His fingers tangled in her hair as he kissed her lips. "I love you, Felicity. And, sure, we haven't talked about this, but you having my baby is the best present you could ever give me. Are you not happy?"

"Of course, I'm happy. Scared but happy."

"We're having a baby!" Liam bellowed again as he tugged her out of the restaurant.

On the drive home, Liam couldn't stop smiling. He was going to be a dad. The woman sitting next to him was his entire world. He'd spend the next hundred years ensuring she had everything she wanted.

Because as long as he had her… Liam had everything.

CHAPTER 30

Nine months later…

"I fucking hate you," Felicity screamed as another contraction hit her.

"Baby… just breathe."

"BREATHE? Are you serious? Let me squeeze your cock, and you tell me how it feels. OH GOD!" She screamed. Squeezing her eyes tightly shut.

"Alright, Felicity, one more push, and your baby will be here." The doctor smiled up at her as he encouraged her to push.

Felicity shook her head. "No… I can't."

"Fels," Liam kissed her cheek, "You can do this. You can do anything. Now, how about you push our kid out so we can meet him or her?" Felicity grunted, squeezing his hand.

"I love you." Liam smiled.

"That's it. Here we go." The doctor grinned.

Felicity felt like her body was splitting in two. She forced herself to keep pushing, and just when she thought she couldn't handle it anymore… she heard the cry of her baby.

The doctor held up a tiny pink baby. "Congratulations, you have a son."

Felicity burst into tears, Liam tugging her into a half hug. "Would you like to cut the cord, Mr. Carver?" Liam leaned down, took the shears from the doctor, and cut the cord. He watched as the doctor handed off his son to the nurse. Felicity was smiling like a megawatt sign.

"Here you go. Mr. and Mrs. Carver, you have a healthy baby boy." They placed the tiny human on his wife's chest.

"He's perfect, baby." Liam kissed her, then his son. "What do you want to name him?"

"Michael Liam Carver."

Liam's eyes filled with tears as he looked at Felicity. She smiled and placed her hand on his cheek. "You saved me, Liam. I was falling into a dark place, and you kept the light shining. I want him to know that his name came from the strongest man I know."

"Baby…" Liam struggled to keep his emotions in check. "Thank you."

FOR THE NEXT couple of hours, Liam watched his wife sleep. His son was cradled in his arms against his chest. He couldn't believe fate had given him the chance to happiness with Felicity again. Even though they'd gone through hell to get where they were, he knew it was worth it.

"Liam?" Felicity stirred, waking from her slumber.

"Hey, baby. I'm right here."

"Where's Michael?" She sat up, smiling, when she saw him bundled in her husband's arms.

Liam stood and scooted next to Felicity on the bed. "Right here." He brushed her hair from her face. "Thank you, Felicity."

Felicity glanced at her husband. "For what?"

"For him… for loving me… for giving me forever." He pressed a kiss to his newborn son's head.

"I should thank you, Liam. I'm the one who didn't deserve a second chance."

"Felicity, that's in the past. What matters is the here and now. And I love you. I love our son."

"I love you." She leaned up and kissed him, pulling Michael from his arms. "My turn."

Liam watched as the woman he'd always loved fed his son. He couldn't wait to get them home and start the rest of their lives. This was precisely what he'd pictured all those years ago when he and Felicity were in school. When she left, she took his heart with her… but now she was here. And even in the face of terror, Felicity still held tight to his heart.

She never really let go.

And neither had he.

Their love had freed them both… *forever*.

143

EPILOGUE

Finn sat at the table, watching Liam swipe the screen on his phone. It was the first time he'd come out for drinks since his wife, Felicity, gave birth to their son. He was undoubtedly a proud parent, and Finn couldn't help being jealous.

He was supposed to have what his friend did, but that crashed and burned when his wife confessed to having an affair. It'd been six months since he packed her shit and signed the papers dissolving their marriage.

"You gonna sit over there and be all moody?" Liam threw a crushed napkin at him.

"Let him be," Chase spoke up. "He's still getting over that bitch of an ex-wife."

Finn shot him a look that said, shut the fuck up. "What?" Chase shrugged. "You know I'm right. Marley wasn't the woman for you, and one day, you'll see that, Finn."

"Well, as real as this has been." Liam stood and tossed some cash on the table. "I'm going home to my wife and son."

"You know what you need?" Hanson smiled. "Some pussy. Seriously—the fastest way to get over someone is to get under them."

Finn snorted. "You are truly an idiot."

"Come on, Sarge. You know that bitch isn't worth the time."

"Yeah… I suppose." Finn fingered the pilsner in his hand as his eyes scanned the bar.

He'd had a few one-night stands since the divorce—hell. Badge bunnies were easy to find. With his looks *and* wallet, he had no trouble in that department. But he wasn't satisfied… not really.

"Awe shit… here comes trouble." Hanson tossed up his hand and waved, causing Finn to turn.

Several firefighters from Station Six strolled through the door like they owned the place. "Hey guys." Alex, the female paramedic, slid into the booth beside Hanson. "Hanson, if you touch me, I'll stab you with this fork." She cut her eyes toward him, and the table erupted into laughter.

Everyone knew Hanson was a pussy magnet—and gave him plenty of shit about it. "Hey now… you know I've got my eyes on someone now. I gotta convince her I'm a catch."

Jason Hunter pulled up a chair. "You mean Becky from the school?"

"Shut up, Captain. Stay away from the school… I don't need your help." Hanson pinned him with a drunken stare.

Jason shook his head. "No, but does it count if they're out in public?"

Hanson leaned over the table. "Where would you run into her if not at the school?"

Jason gave a cocky grin before turning to Hanson. "Here."

Finn and Hanson turned toward the bar. "Holy hell," Finn grumbled before he realized Hanson was standing. Jason was right, she was pretty… but the woman standing with her was fucking gorgeous.

"Who, buddy. Don't storm over there and make an ass of yourself." Finn stood. "I'll go with you. I know Becky and will introduce you as we can get another pitcher."

Finn made his way to the bar, praying like hell Hanson didn't embarrass them both. As soon as he saddled up to the countertop, he was struck with an electric energy that had his skin tingling.

"Hi." He turned to face Becky's friend. "I'm Finn."

Her smile stopped his heart momentarily, but Finn shook it off. "I'm Jenna Hardy." Her voice was like a sweet melody to his soul. Finn was slightly put out by how his body reacted to this woman.

"I don't think I've seen you around." Finn waved the bartender over.

"I've been here two years, but this is the first time I've been to Crimson's."

He found that she'd never been to the most popular bar in Clinton odd but kept the comment to himself. "Oh. Well, I'm a Sergeant on patrol. I'm surprised I haven't crossed paths with you."

"Are you saying I look like a criminal?" She quirked her brow at him, making him laugh.

"No." He smiled again, something he hadn't done in a while. "Though I am good at my job and can usually have someone figured out pretty quickly."

"Full of yourself much?" Jenna sipped her drink and set it down. "If you'll excuse me, I need to use the ladies' room."

Finn sat slack-jawed, watching as the feisty woman stalked toward the bathrooms. His body felt like she'd struck a match and set him on fire. He never reacted this way to his ex-wife, which confused the shit out of him. Needing to see if his reaction was a one-time thing, he got up and headed toward the restrooms, leaving Hanson with Becky at the bar. Jenna was coming out of the bathroom as he rounded the corner into the hallway. Her eyes widened in shock when she saw Finn leaning against the wall as though he was waiting for her.

"Can I help you with something?" Jenna froze as he pushed off the surface and stalked toward her.

Finn couldn't resist. Pausing in front of her, he shoved his fingers into her hair and flattened her body against his. Jenna stiffened at the sudden shock of his lips on hers, but that didn't stop her from fisting his shirt to hold herself steady.

Finn felt the ground shift beneath his feet, threatening to swallow him into a pool of hot, molten desire. His blood lit with an awareness that seemed to scream *more* as he deepened the kiss. Jenna's body melted like languid metal, her once-hard exterior softening as he slipped his tongue into her mouth. The moment seemed to go on forever until Jenna made a throaty noise that had him tearing away from him.

Her head tilted up, and Finn could see she was just as affected by their encounter as he was, so he wasn't expecting her reaction.

Jenna's fisted hands flattened on his chest, and she shoved him—well as best she could. Pushing a man like Finn was no easy feat at her demure stature. Stunned at her sudden change, he stepped back, her absence suddenly felt.

"Jenna." His timber voice rasped out as he reached out to touch her.

But Jenna slapped his hand, her eyes glistening as if she might burst into tears, and shook her head. "No."

"Hey…" She attempted to move away from him, but Finn grabbed her arm. "Wait, *please.*"

"You're a pompous ass, Finn Judson."

And before he could react, Jenna bolted. Finn watched as the feisty woman ran from the bar, leaving him with more questions than answers. Never had he responded to someone the way he did her. Finn reached up and touched his lips, the imprint of Jenna still lingering.

Finn didn't know what to think about her reaction. A part of him felt bad for cornering her and stealing that kiss. But a bigger part of him wanted more.

Finn left the bar after apologizing to Becky for whatever the hell had just happened, his mind in a complete daze. For six months, he walked around angry at women because of what Marley did to him. But with one encounter with the petite brunette, Finn's world was tilted on its axis. He wanted to find her and demand answers.

Jenna Hardy might have run from him… but Finn was patient.

And if there was one thing Finn was confident about—pompous ass or not, was Jenna Hardy was going to end up *his*.

An undeniable connection burns between them… but will the ghosts of their pasts keep them prisoner?
Find out in Signal 69: Holding Jenna

ALSO BY LC TAYLOR

Simply scan the QR code to find your next great read.

Can't scan?

No worries… simply visit

www.behindthebadgepress.com

ABOUT THE AUTHOR

"Grab me a shot of whiskey. These books are about tattooed men and guns!"

What can I say? I'm a down home southern girl who bleeds red, white, and blue, so welcome to My world. I'm an International and USA Today best-selling author, who's an unapologetic down-home southern gal, with a bit of a dirty mouth.

But… I've never met a brooding hero I didn't love. I write my men cut, tattooed and tender, for their down, but-not-out ladies, who just need a little love from the right man.

When I'm not writing my Crossroads Heroes series, creating swoon-worthy love connections, or indulging my darker desires as my alter ego Dori P, I'm curled up with a glass of peach crown and my very own sexy tattooed cop on the couch watching reruns of Chicago Fire..

facebook.com/AuthorLCTaylor

instagram.com/authorlctaylor

bookbub.com/authors/lc-taylor

goodreads.com/authorlctaylor

tiktok.com/NerdyDirtyBookTok

youtube.com/NerdyDirtyBooks

x.com/NerdyDirtyBooks

www.ingramcontent.com/pod-product-compliance
Lightning Source LLC
Chambersburg PA
CBHW060329310726
48976CB00007B/2499